**How could La...
she loved a ma...
out of her life ...years ago...
without a fare-thee-well?**

Would she be able to work with Dake? He had been her husband, for heaven's sake, and now he only asked if they'd met somewhere?

An old familiar ache started in her heart. She had loved him so much. She wished he had not shown up today; it would change everything.

Dear Reader

As spring leads into summer, many people's thoughts turn to holidays. This is an ideal time to look out for our holiday reading pack featuring four exciting stories—all set in the beautiful British countryside. The Yorkshire moors, Scotland, the Isle of Wight and Cornwall will be the glorious backgrounds to these four wonderfully romantic tales. Let us know what you think of them, and of stories set in the UK in general. Would you like more of them, or do you prefer more exotic climates? Do tell.

The Editor

Barbara McMahon, her husband and teenage daughter share their home with one dog and four cats in the San Francisco Bay Area. She works for a computer software company, writing on weekends and evenings. A love for romances and happy endings led to a strong desire to create stories she'd like to read herself. In earlier days she visited exotic locales when she flew for an international airline, and now uses some of these places in her books. Her hobbies are reading, skiing, and writing.

Recent titles by the same author:

ISLAND PARADISE

ONE LOVE FOREVER

BY

BARBARA McMAHON

MILLS & BOON LIMITED
ETON HOUSE   18-24 PARADISE ROAD
RICHMOND   SURREY   TW9 1SR

*First published in Great Britain 1992
by Mills & Boon Limited*

© Barbara McMahon 1992

*Australian copyright 1992
Philippine copyright 1992
This edition 1992*

ISBN 0 263 77608 5

*Set in Times Roman 11½ on 12 pt.
01-9207-43291 C*

Made and printed in Great Britain

CHAPTER ONE

I THOUGHT I'd never see you again...

Lani stared in startled stillness at the man being introduced to their group; she'd thought him gone from her life forever. Her heart began a slow, heavy pounding with the shock of it. The blood roared in her ears, deafening her to the other sounds in the room. She couldn't focus, and she fervently hoped she wasn't going to faint.

Ten years! It had been ten long, endless, lonely years since she had seen him last.

Darting a quick glance around the small group, Lani realised that she had not spoken the words aloud; no one was looking at her in puzzlement— no one was paying any attention to her at all. Every eye was turned to the newcomer.

John Harrington, the company president, made the introductions, moving from person to person, working his way towards her. Before long it would be Lani's turn. She took a deep breath, tried to slow her pounding heart, calm her shattered nerves, to will herself to appear cool, in control, unaffected.

'And this is Lani Williams, our head of communications.' John paused beside her with a smile on his face. 'Lani, meet Dake Morgan.'

The newcomer held out his hand for hers, giving it a brief, formal handshake. His hand was

warm, his fingers firm holding hers. The jolt
from his touch startled her, electrified her. Did
he feel it, too? He gave no outward sign.

She was shocked anew. Staring at him, she
knew it was him, but she saw no recognition in
his glance. No acknowledgement of her at all.

He had matured into a handsome man, tall and
trim, his hair worn a little shorter than when she'd
known him, its colour still a rich dark brown,
untouched by grey.

'Nice to meet you,' he murmured, a polite smile
on his lips.

Lips that had once caused Lani to melt at their
touch, lips that had teased her, loved her, that
once had driven her wild with passion. Now they
only spoke the formal, meaningless phrases of
introduction.

'How do you do?' she replied stiffly, still not
believing what she saw before her. Where had he
been all these years?

As the men moved on, her eyes followed,
unable to look away. Was he real? He had given
no sign of cognisance; had so many years passed
that he didn't recognise her?

Yet he had had time enough to school his features if he'd seen her when he first entered, even
as she had schooled hers. Had he experienced the
same shock as she, an unexpected encounter with
someone from the long ago past? Was he waiting
until they could be alone before acknowledging
her? Would he explain what had happened all
those years ago, want to know what she had been
doing since then?

'Let's take our seats and begin.' John drew out the head chair, motioning to the one on his right for Dake.

Lani took hers, several down and across the table from Dake. The other members of the committee drew their chairs close to the table, notebooks and pencils available, eyes on their leader.

'We're here to discuss the strategy for the new project. It is particularly timely, with Dake joining us now. We're all starting together on this project. As you know, Dake will be picking up Peter's work, so over the next few days each of you will meet with him to brief him on what he needs to know about your area of responsibility, to bring him up to speed. For now, let's turn our energies to the Forscue project.'

As he began his usual opening spiel to the new project, designed to review their company's philosophy, outline the strategy for the task, motivate each of them to high achievements, and briefly review what each of them had heard before, Lani found it hard to concentrate on what John was saying. She'd heard it all many times, of course, but, more importantly, her mind screamed for attention to the problem of Dake Morgan.

What was he *doing* here? How had he come to join the Sanderson Corporation? More importantly, where had he been for the last ten years? Had he ever given her a thought after the day he walked out, never to be seen again by her until today?

For a split second, Lani relaxed her guard. She quickly disciplined her mind. She would *not* think about the past now; there was too much there to bring up. Especially when any minute John would get to the business at hand and she'd have to pay attention.

Another hasty glance at Dake assured her that he was real. He was here, obviously hired as the newest senior vice-president of the Sanderson Corporation. Hired to fill the most important function of the organisation, next to John's. It had been rumoured that Peter was being groomed for the top spot; did that mean Dake was slotted for that position?

The years had treated him well, he had filled out, matured, and he was still devilishly handsome. He wore his expensive Hartman Marx suit with style and flair, but then, he had always liked quality. His graduate degree from Boston University was to be a stepping stone to a good career, one with prestige, a position with money so that he could acquire the quality items he wanted. Always buy the best, he had said; it didn't cost much more and it was always worth the expense. He was in his true milieu now, assured, dynamic, in a position of authority, power and responsibility.

Lani's stomach churned at the thought. She loved Sanderson's. Had devoted years of her life working hard, moving up in the company, contributing to its growth. Dake's coming would change that! Alter the way the company developed, alter the way Lani worked. Did Dake view Sanderson's as a company to grow with and develop as far as he could, or only as a stepping stone to further his own ambitions?

John cleared his throat and sorted the papers before him. Lani shifted her thoughts away from Dake, her mind forcing itself to follow along.

'Now to the new project. Forscue Industries has been threatened with a take-over by Western Forest Products. The offer tendered is capitalising on the series of set-backs Forscue experienced the last few quarters due to changes in legislation regarding the salvaging of forest products. I've had Mark do the financial analysis. Mark.'

Lani drew her packet before her, opening it to find the financial recap. Mark was clear and succinct; he'd done the analysis well, showing where Forscue was weak, how the take-over would affect the stockholders, and the fiscal impact on the market for Forscue products. Clearly, if possible, it would be better long-term to circumvent the take-over. But of course the leveraged buy-out raiders were only interested in short-term gains.

And that was the business of Sanderson Corporation, to provide expert assistance to corporations in danger of take-overs or buy-outs, to help the company managers prevent raiders who moved in motivated solely by quick profits that might endanger the longevity of a company.

Lani had been with Sanderson for eight years. She'd started as a staff assistant, pushed hard to accomplish more, to learn more, working long days, nights, weekends—driving herself to succeed, to get ahead. It had not been easy, but worth it.

She was now director of communications. It was her group that provided the communications the endangered companies used, whether to the media, to stockholders, or to employees. Once Sanderson's started on a project, all communications from the client company were reviewed by Lani or her staff.

Their task was to present the endangered company in the best light possible, discredit where they could the opposing side, instil confidence in employees, the best of whom usually began bailing out when take-over wars were being waged.

She liked her job, liked the work. She'd found a niche where her talents were best used, and everything seemed to be going fine.

Until now.

Now Dake Morgan had joined the corporation, and as a senior vice-president, as well. They'd be constantly thrown together, constantly have to work together. Could they? After all they'd been through together, could they?

As senior vice-president of strategic planning, Dake would spearhead each major project, establish the game plan for each defence, co-ordinate the various functions to ensure the plans meshed smoothly. Being new to the corporation, if not to the business, he'd need extra support from each group, extra time spent reviewing past plans, past successes, hammering out a working one for this defence.

'Any questions?' Mark asked, with his shy smile. He glanced around, nodded and sat down.

Lani dropped her eyes to her notebook. She had let her mind wander again and missed most of Mark's presentation. Darn, she'd have to watch it, she could not afford any mis-steps now. His notes were usually good, though. She would review them closely to make sure she had all the facts. If she'd missed something, she could ask him later.

She needed to pay attention; a true professional wouldn't let a little thing like this upset her. But it was no small thing, her mind screamed.

'Steve, how about the proposed bid?' John motioned to the man sitting beside Dake. Lani's eyes flickered once to Dake, startled to find his dark brown eyes fixed on her, his expression puzzled.

He had always had a habit of looking directly at a person, focusing all his attention on the individual. She looked at Steve, the colour rising in her cheeks. Her heart began beating heavily again as her body exploded into total awareness of Dake Morgan, sitting only a few feet away. She *must* pay attention; she'd have to ignore Dake and remember she was here to work!

The rest of the meeting was hazy to Lani. She found herself repeating each speaker's words in her mind to make sure she focused on what they were saying. She would not permit her thoughts

to wander. She took notes, began thinking of the
best way to publicise what they wanted for
Forscue Industries: letters to stockholders, to
vendors, customers, employees. Some of them
would be standard; most of them would be in-
dividualised for each circumstance.

Time after time her eyes involuntarily flickered
to Dake. More often than not he met her glance,
watching her. Looking away quickly, Lani wanted
all the while to stare at him for endless moments,
to discover what changes had been wrought over
the years, to see if she still found him attractive,
still felt the special magic she'd known before.

At last, the meeting wound down.

'So,' John said, scanning the small group, 'I'll
let Dake get together with each of you over the
next few days, get some ideas going. We'll meet
again, same time next week and see where we
stand, how far we've got. We need to move
quickly on this one. Now, where do we stand with
the Sorenson deal?'

The rest of the meeting sped by as each person
provided status updates of where their group
stood on the various ongoing projects.

Lani was exhausted by the time she reached
her office. The shock of seeing Dake, the strain
of trying to ignore him when every nerve clamoured for his attention, was tiring. Her hands
were shaky, her knees weak. She had to get
control before she met him alone.

There was still half an hour before her normal
quitting time, though her secretary had already
left for the day. Enough time to read the rest of

her mail, maybe dictate that memo for Judy, and then call it a day. She needed to get busy—time enough to think of Dake Morgan when she got home.

Lani was almost through her pile of mail when the encounter she'd been half expecting, half dreading, happened.

'Lani, isn't it?' Dake stood in her doorway, his smile easy, friendly, disturbing.

She looked up, colour flooding her cheeks, happiness spilling into her heart in spite of herself. He was tall, he always had been, but he'd filled out from the days when she'd known him, though he was still lean and trim, with long legs, wide shoulders. His face had aged a little and there was a thin scar along one temple. She had not noticed it earlier. His eyes were still a warm dark brown, with long thick lashes, his hair dark and thick. God, he looked good!

'Yes.' He knew who she was; what was he playing at?

'As John said, we need to talk, have you bring me up to date.'

She nodded. At least they were spared the others being privy to their meeting.

'Yes, I know, but not here, not now.'

'It is getting late. How about I buy us a drink and you can fill me in a little?'

'Fill you in?' she enquired, puzzled. Did he mean tell him everything she'd been doing for the last ten years, over a drink?

'Let me know the general way you set about planning the communication campaign, what's worked well in the past, what you're thinking of for this one.'

He stood easily in the doorway, not self-conscious, not mysterious, the Forscue folder clearly in his hand.

He was talking about *business*!

'I've already made plans for this evening,' Lani said slowly, wondering when he would bring up their past, waiting for him to do so. Vowing she'd not be the one to do it. She had not left; he had.

'Can't you cancel?'

Slowly she shook her head. She wouldn't even if she'd had something planned. Once she would have done anything he asked, just for the chance to make him happy. No more.

He shrugged. 'Another time, maybe. What's your schedule like tomorrow?'

Glancing at her calendar, she replied briskly, 'I'm free from nine-thirty till noon. Any time then would be fine.'

'I'll see you at nine-thirty.' He gave her a long look, his eyes narrowing. 'Have we met before?' he asked.

'I'm sure I would remember if I'd met you before,' she answered, shuffling papers on her desk.

'I don't know, there's something nagging in the back of my mind... Oh, well, it'll come to me. Goodnight, Lani.'

She looked up as he walked away, numb. *It'll come to me!* He had filled her thoughts for years, still haunted her dreams at night, and he couldn't even remember her! Had their association been so meaningless to him that he couldn't even place her face? Had she changed so much through the years that he couldn't place her name? It had been Dake who had first called her Lani. She had been Melanie all her life until Dake had shortened it. One of the legacies from their association together, she'd kept Lani, hoping it would, somehow, bring him back. Stupid, superstitious nonsense. And if he was back, what was she going to do?

Lani stood shakily and grabbed her bag. She was leaving. She'd finish her mail in the morning. It was time she sought the safety of her home.

She drove swiftly through the homebound traffic of Boston, her nerves soothed by the ride along the Charles River, despite the heavy traffic. It was one of her favourite places, with the lights from Cambridge reflecting on the water as she sped to pick up her daughter.

Annalise's baby-sitter greeted Lani at the door, as a small bundle of energy ran up to hug her. Lani held her tightly for only a moment. She couldn't give way now—Annalise was too quick; she'd pick up that something was wrong if Lani acted out of character.

'Hi, Mom, you're early. I'll be ready in a sec. I had a great day in school, and Mrs Palmer and I baked cookies, too.' Giving her mother another quick hug, she dashed across the room to gather her books.

'How are you doing, Ms Williams? Going on vacation soon?' Mrs Palmer asked as they waited for Annalise to get her homework packed up.

'We're still planning on Christmastime. A new project just came in, hope it won't interfere. Ready, honey?'

Lani gazed fondly at her daughter, searching for any resemblance to her father. Annalise had Dake's dark hair and square jaw. The rest of her daughter's features resembled her, from her grey eyes to the slight dimple in her left cheek that flashed when she smiled.

Lani had studied her daughter from birth, always looking for signs of her father, only finding them in her colouring and in the strong line of her jaw. Probably just as well. She loved her daughter but was not sure she could stand to be forcibly reminded of Dake every time she looked at her. She was reminded tonight, however. An old ache tugged her heart.

Bidding the baby-sitter goodbye, they drove the short distance to their apartment.

Lani parked in the garage, pride in her home swelling within her heart. Purchased just last year, when she'd been promoted to director, it was perfect for the two of them, with two bedrooms, a large living-room, dining-room and a kitchen with every gadget and convenience available. To Lani it represented success, once an elusive, far-off dream. She loved it.

Her home was her refuge, her retreat. She socialised very little with the people from work, keeping her personal life separate from her professional one. She did not talk much about her daughter, did not talk about her past at all. She was at work to work, at home to live as she chose.

'What's for dinner?' Annalise asked as they entered the blue and white kitchen.

'Spaghetti, OK?' Lani smiled; she knew the answer to that!

'Super, with garlic bread, too?'

'Yes. Put up your books, wash your hands and you can do the bread. I'll change and start the spaghetti.'

Lani lingered over dinner, talking with Annalise about her day, listening with love as her daughter enthusiastically described the antics she and her friends had been involved in. Taking her time, she worked with Annalise on the rest of her homework, in no hurry to finish the task. She knew as soon as she was alone, once Annalise was in bed, the memories would come. She'd not be able to keep them at bay any longer. And Lani wanted to, as long as she could.

Finally her daughter was asleep, the apartment tidy, the inevitable about to happen.

Where should she even begin? The bright, shining days when they first met; the endless happy hours they had spent together; their last day together? Or the long dark years that followed?

Lani didn't want to remember any of it. The happy days mocked her with their outcome, the dark years were a constant burden of sadness and heartache, a twisting of love gone.

She should remember the bad years, guard against it ever happening to her again. She was not so naïve, so trusting now. She would guard against the false bright promise of undying love, go her way alone.

Yet all could have been alleviated, had Dake only cared enough.

She had not expected to see him today. She had never expected to see him again. She'd known John was interviewing someone to replace Peter, but she had been out of town lately with the meeting in Washington on the Sorenson matter. She had been gone the week the various candidates had visited their offices and met the other division heads. Too caught up in last-minute deadlines when she returned to talk with fellow employees about the candidates, who they were, where they were from. She had been remiss in not following up.

What was Dake doing at Sanderson's? She would have thought he'd have gone to New York and found a high-paying, high-power position. Yet here he was in Boston, and at Sanderson's.

What had he been doing over the last ten years? Had he been in Boston all those years? Had he thought of her at all?

And she, how could she have ever married a man who would just up and walk out on her? How could she ever have thought she loved a man who gave no concern to what was happening to her, who had walked out of her life ten years ago without a fare-thee-well? It was over, long ago.

Would she be able to work with him, be cordial and respectful, when all the time she hated what he'd done? Would always have that between them?

He had been her husband, for heaven's sake, and now he only asked if they'd met somewhere?

An old familiar ache started in her heart. She had loved him so much, ten years ago. She wished he had not shown up today; it would change everything.

CHAPTER TWO

LANI spent a sleepless night reliving the past, trying to find where she'd gone wrong, or what she could have done to have things turn out differently. It was a topic she'd explored many endless times, always with the same result: she didn't know why Dake had walked out on her, never to return. It had seemed out of character, but then, she had known him for such a short time—what was his true character?

They had met in the autumn, had a whirlwind courtship and secretly married at Christmas. He was gone in April. Sometimes it seemed like a dream. Except for the heartbreak she experienced. And Annalise.

Lani dressed with care the next morning. Her light brown hair was neatly confined to a French plait, make-up lightly applied. She was the picture of a successful, confident businesswoman. She loved her dark charcoal-grey wool suit, and the snowy white silk blouse gave just the hint of femininity she wanted. She knew it was a power suit and she needed every ounce of power she could muster this day. It would get easier; everything did, eventually. But for today she needed all the confidence she could garner.

Seeing Dake every day would have to get easier, or she would have to find another job. And she didn't want to do that; she had worked too hard where she was to start over somewhere else. Surely after all this time she could treat Dake as a new acquaintance, a stranger.

The man she thought she knew no longer existed, probably never had. After a few months of playing house with the naïve student from Pennsylvania, he had taken off. Shedding the responsibilities of a family like a snake shed his skin. It was an apt comparison, she thought grimly.

Dropping Annalise at school, Lani arrived at work only a few minutes earlier than normal. As she passed Peter's old office, now Dake's, she felt a twinge of sadness. Peter had been so good to her, for her, and she missed him dreadfully.

He and Mattie had been planning to retire in the southern states, where they could enjoy the warm weather and travel. The heart attack had been swift and deadly and now he was gone for good. She missed him. It would have been bad enough when he retired next year, but she could have called him, reviewed things with him, heard his opinions on issues. Now she felt alone, adrift.

And to top things off, she had the added worry of dealing with Dake Morgan. How would Peter have advised her on that?

'Good morning, Lani.' Dake spoke behind her. She'd recognise that voice anywhere, deep, resonant, capable of seductive undertones in the heart of the night. She turned to face him, not expecting to see him this early. They were to meet at nine-thirty. She needed more time to get ready.

'Good morning; you're in early.' She felt like a nervous student again, not the successful businesswoman she had become. And suddenly she resented him for making her feel so vulnerable.

'Guess I will be in early for a while, there's so much to catch up on, to learn. I want to start pulling my weight as soon as I can. I know John said to plan on time for a reasonable learning curve, but I want to cut it down.'

She nodded. He had always been impatient, wanting to cut right to the bottom of things, push for accomplishments. In that he hadn't changed.

'Well, I won't keep you,' she said as he drew near.

'You're not keeping me; one of the best ways to find out things is to discuss them with the others on the staff. You've been here a long time, right?'

Lani licked her lips as he stopped before her. His eyes were warm and direct, gazing intently down at her as if what she said was of monumental importance to him. His head was angled slightly as he waited for her reply. His dark grey three-piece suit fitted him like a glove, with the pale blue shirt and Paisley tie accentuating his good looks.

Ten years ago, the only time she had seen him in a suit was the day they were married; the rest of the time it had been jeans.

He no longer looked like the wild and fun-loving graduate student she had known. He looked distinguished, successful, authoritative. He was over six feet tall, a head taller than she was. She resented his superior height. She resented his success. She had to struggle to get where she was. He had made it too, but with any struggle?

His gaze changed, his expression grew puzzled.

'Darn it, but you remind me of someone. I can't think who, but there's something——'

'Dake, I came in early to get caught up on my mail. I'll...we'll get together at nine-thirty as planned, OK?'

She opened her office door and moved quickly to her desk. Her legs were trembling and she didn't want him to notice how her knees were shaking. She heard him concur, heard his steps move down the hall as she sank gratefully into her chair, gripping the edge of her desk.

Tears welled in her eyes, and she impatiently dashed them away. The past was gone. Let it go. Things would not be like that again. But he looked good. The old desire rose, Lani firmly put it down.

She had a couple of hours to get a hold of herself. She couldn't go on like this or she'd wind up a basket case. Every time she looked at him she was torn between screaming, 'Why did you leave me?' and throwing herself into his arms to beg him to come back.

Did he really not remember her, or was his line about her reminding him of someone just an opening for her to initiate the revelation? How could he not remember her? Had he married dozens of women?

She had never stopped thinking about him, had
had no trouble recognising him the moment he
had entered that conference-room. But it appeared he hadn't given her a thought in all these
years.

She rummaged around on her desk until she
found her thick reading-folder. Stacey, her secretary, put all reading memos and letters in this
file, the information-only items, ones not needing
a reply from Lani. She knew this file would have
the dossier on Dake Morgan, the one she could
have read before now. The one that would have
indicated he was a candidate.

Could she have swayed the decision to hire
Dake had she known earlier? Could she have
found anything which would have raised doubts
in John's mind and changed the hiring decision?
Too late now.

She found the papers and, darting a quick
glance out to the hall to make sure he'd left, she
began to read. It was brief, concise and impressive. He had only included the last ten years'
experience, no educational information, but his
rise out of the financial houses in Chicago had
been remarkable. He himself had at one time in-
itiated leverage buy-outs. Now he worked against
them. Nothing like a convert for knowledge and
experience.

She closed the folder. John had chosen well in
Dake Morgan. Nothing she could have said could
counter that.

Lani reached for her mail.

'Sorry I'm late.' Dake breezed into her office, a thick folder in one hand, a notebook and pencil in the other. He had shed his jacket but still looked the successful executive in his pale blue shirt with the charcoal waistcoat.

Lani looked up, then glanced at the clock on her desk. It was nine-fifty.

'No problem, I didn't realise how late it was.' She pushed the spreadsheet away and arched her back to ease her shoulder muscles. Looking up at Dake, she blushed when she saw his gaze at the taut material across her breasts. She immediately sat up straight and the material eased.

He grinned at her, not at all embarrassed to be caught staring.

'Now a good time?' he asked.

'For what?' She felt suddenly tongue-tied, stupid.

'To review the game plan for the Forscue project, what else?' His eyes glinted, daring her to suggest something else. He drew the visitor chair to her side of the desk.

'As good as any,' she murmured, drawing her own project folder out, inching her chair away from his. He was too close; she couldn't concentrate. A thousand questions tumbled in her brain.

'I understand you were close to Peter McDonald,' Dake said, not missing the retreat.

'Yes. Peter was a good man—I guess you could say he was my mentor. He taught me a lot. I miss him.'

'He seems to have been organised, practical and creatively brilliant.'

Lani thawed a little towards Dake, glad he had recognised that fact in a man no longer present, in the position he was now filling. She was struck with the thought that Dake had nothing to prove. He could give credit where due and still feel comfortable taking over. He was no longer the brash, cocky college student, but a mature man, sure of himself, confident in his abilities. Lani was intrigued.

'I thought Peter was great,' she said quietly.

'So did John. He's a tough act to follow. I won't be like him, Lani—can't be. I don't think we should start with any false assumptions. I will do things differently, if for no other reason than that I'm a different person. I don't want animosity with you or anyone else here because of it.'

'You won't get it from me. I may not agree with everything you propose, but if it's determined that it's in the best interest of the company, I'll support it one hundred per cent. I didn't always agree with Peter, you know.'

'And the others?'

'Don't see things that aren't there. Peter died almost two months ago. We all knew that would cause major changes. We're looking for someone to do the job, not fill Peter's shoes.'

Dake smiled, the lines near his eyes deepening as if he smiled often. His teeth were strong and white, his face slightly tanned. Odd, so late in the year; had he been in the south before coming here, a quick vacation before starting the new job?

'Would you know me again?' he asked softly, that disturbing glint in his eye.

Lani looked away, realising she'd been staring. 'Sorry, I was speculating on your tan.'

She turned back to the folder. The last thing she should be doing was speculating on anything about Dake Morgan.

'I took a long weekend in Orlando, got plenty of sun. It'll fade soon, though. Now to the Forscue project. What exactly does your group do on projects of this nature?'

Lani spent the next two hours with Dake reviewing all aspects of her job, and those of the people who worked for her. Explaining how they assessed the corporate culture of each firm, how they tailored the communications needs to the particular situation. Dake's questions were well thought out; he quickly grasped what she was accomplishing and offered one or two suggestions she respected.

'Do you ever do site work?' he asked at one point.

'Oh, yes, that's crucial, I think, to getting a firm grasp of the individual corporate culture. I can't just listen to what the senior management tells me. It will be slanted from their point of view. I visit all offices of a corporation to get the feel for how the employees view themselves and their company. It's from that that I really do most of the positioning of the articles, communiqués and so on.'

'I think it would benefit all aspects of the proposed buy-out defence if all the key people here did so.'

'We all try to, early in the project, and make a second visit as we progress, if at all feasible. It's more important for you as the project leader to do so, less so for Mark or Joel, but we all try to visit at least once. Sometimes other priorities pop up and prevent it.'

His hands toyed with his pencil as he watched Lani talk. The motion drew Lani's eyes.

She was aware of his hands, with their long slender fingers, hands that had once rubbed her back when she'd been tired from painting their apartment; hands that had gently strapped her sprained ankle when she had fallen while ice skating; hands that had caressed her, brought her to ecstasy and beyond. She looked away with an effort, her gaze moving to his face.

She wondered about the thin scar that ran from his hair-line down to the top of his cheek, just missing his temple. What had caused it? Had it hurt much? She felt shut out of his life, as she had from the day he'd left.

He had been fun, romantic, daring. The perfect husband, or so she had thought.

Water under the bridge, Lani told herself firmly, looking back at her notes.

The time sped by, and Lani grew relaxed. She was in her element talking about her work. She loved it and it showed. She was knowledgeable in her field, and in what she did for Sanderson.

Dake would find no reason to think her area weak.

Lani glanced at her clock; time had flown. Dake was reviewing his notes, his pencil tapping a rhythm as he scanned the last page. Lani became mesmerised by its rhythm. It was a habit he had had when they'd studied together. The business discussion had driven out all thoughts of the past, but this unconscious habit recalled it sharply, vividly.

She was instantly transported back to the little one-bedroom apartment they had shared overlooking the Charles River, near the university. The lights had been bright in their small living-room, so they could read and study. Together at their rickety table they'd have their papers spread out, their books and notes, lost in thought, or study. Then the tapping of Dake's pencil would penetrate her concentration and she would stop. He wasn't aware he was doing it and would go on forever until she cleared her throat.

Looking up, he would become aware, grin sheepishly. 'Sorry, love.' A quick kiss and back they'd go to studying. And he'd keep the pencil quiet for another hour or so.

The tapping continued. Unconsciously, Lani cleared her throat. Dake looked up, startled. He looked at her, but she didn't think he saw her: he was looking beyond her, at something that wasn't there. Had he remembered, too?

'Dake?' she said softly.

'Sorry, I had a fleeting . . . never mind. I guess that wraps it up. How about lunch?'

'No,' she said, too quickly. 'I mean, I'm busy. I already have plans.' She foundered around for a graceful way to get out of lunch without seeming rude. Now she'd have to go out somewhere, just so he wouldn't know she was trying to avoid him. Damn, why did he have to have come to Sanderson's anyway?

'Another time, then.' He gathered his papers and replaced her visitor's chair. 'Thanks for all the info. Once you have those proposals you were talking about, let me know; I'd like to see them.'

'Sure, tomorrow or Thursday.'

Lani watched him leave and sat back in her chair, feeling drained but triumphant. She'd done it! She'd pulled it off, sitting for two hours with him, maintaining a totally professional attitude! She could do it; she could forget he was the husband that had walked out on her and treat him just like another business colleague. It would work, as long as she kept it strictly professional. As long as she did not let her thoughts fly back in time.

But at what cost? She was exhausted; it had taken every bit of self-control she possessed to maintain her calm demeanour. She was tired, but satisfied. She had proved to herself she could finally put the past behind her.

Lani rose and stretched, dropping her arms quickly when she remembered the way Dake had looked at her this morning. She'd better become more circumspect.

She'd take a break for lunch, go over to Faneuil Hall and lose herself among the tourists for a time; forget all about Dake Morgan. She would come back to work refreshed.

During the afternoon Lani tried to concentrate on her proposal, but found her attention wandering, listening for Dake's footsteps, wondering if he'd return. Twice he passed her office, but didn't stop. Not that she wanted him to stop; he was already occupying too much of her attention. The day suddenly seemed endless.

As she was leaving, she had to pass his office. Not wanting to stop and talk, but only to escape, she paused just before his door, drew a deep breath and walked briskly past, calling a quick goodnight.

He called to her, but she ignored him and practically ran to her car. She knew she was being a coward, but she dreaded bringing up their mutual past. Was he biding his time to talk to her, to bring it up later, when it suited him?

She didn't want to know, now, why he'd left her. Didn't want to hear his excuses. She wanted to forget the past and only look to the future. Maybe he felt the same way. What good would it do to rehash what had happened? It wouldn't change anything. It was as it was, and discussing it would not change it.

But, a small voice nagged, wouldn't you really like to know why he left? What he's being doing for ten years?

The next morning Lani reached her office without running into Dake. He was in; she knew by the open office, the papers on his desk. She, however, didn't see him. She did her work, hoping to avoid him all day.

The morning was well advanced when Lani went to Joel Perkins' office for some graphics he was designing for her. He was casual, and wanted to shoot the breeze before settling down to business. Lani perched on his desk, matching his banter with her own.

'Come on, Lani, say yes, just this once.' Joel smiled up at Lani as he rocked back in his chair behind his desk. She leaned back on her hands, smiling as she shook her head.

'Joel, you've been asking me for months. I always say no. Why do you keep on?'

He was fun to be around at work, but there was no point in misleading him; she was not interested in dating.

He rose and moved to stand near her, a tall man, just over six feet tall, fair and carefree. Lani became silent as she found herself comparing him with Dake. There was no magic with Joel as there had been with Dake.

'I'll overwhelm you with my passion. You'll beg for me to take you out and have my way with you.' He leered at her in fun.

She laughed. 'You goose, your passion would be wasted. The answer——'

A throat was cleared. Startled, both turned guiltily to face the door. Lani froze when she saw Dake in the doorway. The smile slowly faded from her face and she sat up, eased herself to the edge of the desk. What did Dake think of the scene?

'Hope I'm not interrupting,' he said, his voice expressionless, his eyes hard.

Joel's smile broadened. 'Not at all. Maybe you can help me, as head of strategic planning and all. I'm trying to get this hard-headed young woman to go out with me to a Patriots' game next weekend, but she keeps refusing. Should I alter my strategy?'

His manner was brisk, breezy. Not for him the undercurrents of suspicion, the doubts and years of loneliness behind him.

'No liking for football?' Dake asked as he moved into the office, his eyes never leaving Lani.

'No liking for brash young men who try blackmail,' she said lightly, hopping off the desk.

Perhaps it had been a mistake; she was caught neatly between the two tall men and her whole body focused on Dake Morgan, nerve-endings quivering to be soothed by his touch. The two of them could have been alone, for all the awareness she had of Joel. She swallowed hard.

'Blackmail?' Dake raised an eyebrow.

'No such thing,' Joel stoutly defended. 'Just overwhelming her with my charm, sweeping her off her feet, so to speak.'

She was aware of the light scent of Dake's aftershave, musky and tantalising, the same brand he'd worn when she'd known him before. It turned her insides to mush. She remembered the scent lingering on her own skin when they'd made love, how she loved to rest her cheek on his shoulder and trace her fingers across his chest as his breathing slowed to normal. Wrapped in love and all that went with it.

She blinked. Thoughts like that were dangerous.

'Are you all right?' Dake asked, his expression changing to one of concern.

'Of course.' Lani turned to Joel, a scathing look upon her face. 'I tried that once, remember? It didn't work. I've got work to do, Joel; are you finished with that graphic design for Montgomery or not?'

'I'll have it to you by noon.'

Lani nodded, and tried to ease around Dake. He side-stepped in front of her. 'It's you I'm looking for.'

She looked up at him, a sinking sensation in her stomach, her eyes wide, her skin paling a little. All she wanted to do was escape, have some time to herself.

'John said you'd be the best to update me on the Sorenson matter. Looks as if we might be needed again before the Security and Exchange Commission.'

'Not again! God, I was there for weeks,' she groaned. 'What now?'

'I'll catch you in your office in a couple of minutes, let you know what I know.'

'OK.' She started towards the door, turning to smile at Joel. 'Thanks anyway, huh?'

'Sure, maybe next time.'

'You're hopeless.' She smiled at him, avoided Dake's eyes and left. As Lani walked slowly down the hall she could hear Dake's question.

'What did she mean, she'd tried that and it hadn't worked?'

Joel's response was muffled, but Lani knew what he'd say. The office knew she was a single parent, that she had no husband living with her. Probably everyone knew, too, that she didn't date. It wasn't a secret, just not something she talked about often. Now Dake would know. Would it matter? Would he feel guilty for causing it, or wonder why she didn't?

How long would it be before she and Dake sat down and brought everything out in the open? Her own curiosity was strong; what had he been doing over the years? Why had he returned to Boston? Didn't he want to know anything about her? Had their association meant so little to him that he didn't even care to ask how the years had treated her? Her heart ached at that thought.

'About the Sorenson matter.' Dake was framed in her doorway.

She looked up from the report she was trying to read, suddenly wishing he'd stride in, slam the door behind him and sweep her up in his arms, demanding she give them another chance. Wishing he'd beg her forgiveness for deserting her so long ago, promise lifelong devotion if she'd only give him another chance.

But would she? Would she ever put herself in such a vulnerable position again? She couldn't trust him. That he'd changed and would come back to her was the essence of fairy-tales, happy ever after. He'd already proved he wasn't a stayer.

She knew where she was now, no more foolish fantasies.

'Are you OK?' he asked again.

She blinked. He was standing in the doorway with a curious expression on his face, but not one of contrition or passion.

'The Sorenson matter—you said there may be more problems with it?' she said, ignoring his question, flushing at her thoughts.

'According to John, he just got a letter this morning asking for more assistance in further hearings before the SEC. He said I should talk to you—you were in on the earlier meetings.'

'Yes, and I thought our part was done. The SEC is investigating possible fraud on the proposed take-over bid by A.I.L. International for Sorenson. We had information that supported Sorenson, so were called to testify.'

'You're the one who was in Washington when I was interviewed. That's why we didn't meet until I started.' He sank casually into the visitor's chair.

'I was at the hearings. I knew interviews were being conducted here, but couldn't get back.' She bit her lip; she should have found out about the candidates before. It was silly—by ignoring the process she'd been acting as if it weren't true, as if Peter weren't gone for good.

But he was gone, and she should have faced the reality of it sooner.

But would it have made any difference? Would any input from her have altered the final decision? What could she have objected to? His credentials were impressive, his experience perfect for the position.

'It looks as if we'll have to go down to Washington again, at least for a couple of days.'

'We? I went alone last time. I handled it fine.'

Dake shrugged. 'No challenge intended. John thought it might help me to get on top of that project if I was included. You'd still be the spokesman—er—spokesperson.'

'You don't need to use generic names on my account; I'm not sensitive,' Lani said stiffly, more worried about the prospect of their travelling together than sexist titles.

'Since we missed the interview, perhaps you'd like another chance. How about dinner on Friday?' Dake asked, leaning back comfortable in the chair.

She shook her head automatically. 'Sorry...'

'I know—busy. You're the busiest person I've met recently. How much ahead would I have to book to get you?'

'Lani, Mr Carmichael is on line three. It's his second call this morning; he really needs to talk to you.' Stacey's voice rang on the intercom.

Thankfully, Lani reached for her phone.

'You can let me know the answer later,' Dake said with a sardonic smile. He'd recognised her delaying tactics, her relief at the timely interruption.

As Lani took the call, she knew she'd have to respond at some time. Either face him, or tell him why she couldn't. She would put the moment off as long as she could. She didn't like awkward confrontations.

CHAPTER THREE

LANI took all steps she could during the next week to isolate herself from Dake Morgan. She avoided him wherever possible, and arranged for her secretary to call her when she went into meetings so she'd have to leave early and not be caught by him afterwards.

She devoted herself to working on her projects, often working behind closed doors in order to avoid interruption. She followed her staff closely, to make sure all their assignments were in on time. She did not want to give Dake any excuse to seek her out.

When the inevitable meetings took place, she was abrupt, and quick to leave. It was only thus that she was able to hold on to her tenuous control. At one meeting, Dake asked her to visit the site of Forscue Industries, to get the impressions she needed for effective communications. She accepted the assignment readily. It would take her out of the office for a week. Just what she could use.

Fortunately Mrs Palmer was used to taking care of Annalise overnight, or longer when Lani went on short trips, even with short notice. There would be no problem there.

By the end of the second week, Lani convinced herself that she could stay at her job, that she was becoming inured to Dake's presence, accustomed to the idea that he would not bring up their joint past if she didn't.

The question never far from her mind was: did she want to bring it up? It appeared he genuinely didn't remember her. It had been ten years, and she had changed both physically and emotionally. Perhaps he really didn't remember her. That thought brought a twinge of pain, however, for she'd remembered every hour they had spent together. Even if he felt nothing for her, she wished he had remembered their younger selves.

Lani frequently re-read the dossier the company had prepared at the time of the interview as if it would give her the answers she was seeking. It indicated that Dake had never been married. She had stared at it a long time when she first read it. Was that false, or had theirs only been a sham wedding?

Her aunt Polly had always thought it was not a real marriage. Had she been right? Had Dake thought that the only way to have her was to fake a marriage? It had been a secret because of complications with his grant, or so he had told her. All these years when she'd thought she had been married, had it only been an illusion?

'Mr Harrington's called a meeting in the main conference-room in ten minutes.' Stacey's voice broke into Lani's thoughts.

She flipped the knob on the intercom. 'Thanks, I'll be there. What's it on, do you know?'

'The Forscue project, I think.'

Lani gathered her folders and set off for the conference-room.

'Western Forest Products are moving more aggressively than we originally thought they would. The issue is heating up and I think we need to move swiftly to counter the attack. Dake will review his assessment with you; we'll discuss it and come to a plan today. Once outlined, we will move with all speed to implement it.'

Lani switched her attention to Dake as he outlined his strategic plan to thwart the take-over bid. He presented his views well, without excess or flowery words. He cut to the heart of the matter, listing each step and phase to be undertaken.

Lani thought once, briefly, of Peter. He had been more methodical, more deliberate, but he would have liked Dake's presentation.

Dake was forceful, convincing, precise, and his ideas were good. What was more, his timetable was aggressive enough to combat the opposition. The outcome was still up in the air, but Lani thought their chances of winning were improved.

'Lani is visiting the plants and the corporate office next week. I know it's short notice, but I think we need to strike fast on communications, especially on internal communications.

'Mark, you'll have to get those adjusted figures to me before Monday. I'm going with Lani and want to take them with me. Steve, can you ...?'

Lani's eyes opened wide in startled realisation. Dake was going with her; she had not known that. She swallowed hard, her heart pounding. She didn't want him to go with her! She had been dreading the possibility of his going with her to Washington for the committee hearings, but that would have been a quick trip down and back, with the meetings occupying all their time. The Forscue corporate office was in California, a five-hour plane ride, in addition to the time it would take to drive out to the offices. Their plant was located miles from the nearest airport, in the Sierra Nevada mountain range. More hours in a car, just the two of them.

She couldn't do it. She just couldn't. She would have to find a way to say no.

'Lani, you and I'll review the final format before we go.' Dake looked at her strangely.

She nodded, numb to what was going on. She'd have to tell him she couldn't go, he would have to get someone else. But not in front of all the others; she'd tell him later, privately.

Later never came. Thursday and Friday sped by. Where Lani had once tried to avoid Dake, she now felt he was avoiding her. They were due to leave on Monday, but she couldn't get in to see him to tell him she couldn't go; he was either in meetings, or on the phone, or had 'just left'.

Finally, desperately, on Friday afternoon she wrote him a short note, telling him she would not be able to go but she would send Margot, one of her lead assistants, instead. Slipping it into his 'in' box before she left, she tried to consider the matter closed. It bothered her that she was falling down on her job; she'd never done so before.

But then the circumstances had never been quite like this before.

Annalise greeted her enthusiastically when Lani picked her up.

'No homework this weekend, Mom; great, huh? You didn't forget I'm going to Judith-Ann's to sleep over tonight, did you?'

'No, sweetie, I didn't forget. If your room is tidy, as soon as we've finished dinner, you can go.'

'It is; I cleaned it last night, remember? We're renting movies and going to watch them all night!'

Lani smiled at her daughter. She was the delight of her life, made everything worthwhile. 'So I can expect you home late tomorrow morning?'

'We might not get up until noon. Will you be home next Friday night, in case I want to have Judith-Ann stay with us?'

'I will. I changed my plans to go on my trip. Darn, which reminds me, I'd better call Mrs Palmer when I get home. I'm not going now, and forgot to let her know.'

Lani had mentioned the trip to her baby-sitter when Dake had first approached her. Now she needed to tell her it was off.

'I'm glad you'll be home. Maybe Judith-Ann and you and me can make cookies next Friday.'

'Sure, why not?' Making a mental note to call Mrs Palmer, Lani asked Annalise how her day in school had gone.

The apartment was quiet when she returned from dropping Annalise off at Judith-Ann's. The evening loomed ahead of her. Changing into dark brown wool trousers and a cream sweater, she built a fire in the fireplace and drew her briefcase towards her. If the Sorenson matter was looming again, she'd review her notes on it. Better to be prepared, she always found.

It was after eight when the doorbell rang. Lani frowned, her concentration interrupted. Who could it be? It wasn't quite the end of the month, too early for the paper-boy.

She opened the door to find Dake Morgan standing on her porch, dressed in dark cords, a navy turtleneck, and a heavy suede jacket, briefcase in hand.

'Hi, I hoped you would be home. I came to see you,' he said, an easy smile on his face.

She stepped back as he moved confidently into the room. Closing the door, she watched him silently as he surveyed her living-room. Quickly she scanned the area to see if there were any signs of Annalise. Thankfully there were none, and she was gone for the night.

Dake took in the cosy fireplace, the comfortable sofa and chairs, the pleasing combination of blues, whites and light browns. He nodded to the table with her work.

'What are you, some kind of workaholic like me?'

'Just going over a few things,' she murmured. 'Why did you come?'

'To talk to you.'

Was this it? Would they at last talk about themselves? Lani felt sick inside; she didn't want to talk about it, she wanted him to leave.

Without waiting to be asked, he moved to the sofa and sat down. She followed slowly, sitting gingerly, on edge, at the other end, watching him warily.

'I've come about the Forscue project,' he began.

'I'm not going,' she said quickly. Damn, she still hadn't called Mrs Palmer. She would do that, as soon as Dake left.

'I got your damn-fool note. What did you mean by that?'

'Margot is good, she can go in my place.'

'If I'd wanted some assistant, I'd have asked for one. What I wanted was another high-level person from the company; I want to show Forscue and Western Forest Products that we have our highest people on this one. Are you afraid of flying?'

'Flying? No, I fly all over.' She was confounded by his question.

'You've been out on other on-site visits before, and if you're not afraid of flying, it must be me you object to travelling with. You used to go with Peter, didn't you?'

'Yes.' His logic was superb; he had hit the nail on the head.

'So why the note? Why not just tell me?'

'I couldn't get in to see you. The trip's Monday, and I had no other way to let you know.

You've been avoiding me ever since Wednesday's meeting.'

'That's rich. I have the distinct feeling you are *always* avoiding me. Why don't you want to go with me?'

Lani's mouth was dry. She couldn't tell him, yet she had to say something. He'd not let it lie there.

'Do you dislike me?' he pushed.

She shook her head. *Au contraire*, she realised with a shock. She must never let him know it.

'I'm not Peter.'

'No, you're not.'

'What is it, Lani? Tell me! I can't work through it if I don't know.' Frustration tinged his voice.

She licked her lips. 'I don't want to go with you,' she said at last.

'Hell, I know that, but why?'

She looked into the fire, ill at ease, at a loss as to what to say next. Dake moved along the sofa until he was close to her. She was afraid to turn her head, afraid to see how close he was. Her heart was pounding so hard she knew he must see it, must hear it. She wished she had a drink of water to wet her throat.

'Lani.'

She reluctantly turned to face him, her eyes drawn to his lips, firm and chiselled above a strong chin. Those same lips that had once kissed her, awakening her to delights never dreamed of. The lips that had moved her to passion, lips that had trailed paths of fire across her cheeks, down her throat, caressing the mounds of her breasts.

She felt as if he had touched her again with the warmth and tenderness he'd once shown. His mouth a heady intoxication, a wild delight to be savoured and repeated.

'God, Lani, when you look at me like that I have a hard time remembering this is a business relationship and that we are business associates. I wouldn't change the rules, unless you want it.'

'No!'

She sprang up from the sofa, escaping his proximity, moving to stand before the fire, gazing down into it as if it held all the answers. She didn't have time to draw breath before he was there beside her, his hands on her shoulders, forcing her to face him.

'Lani, I'm not some ogre about to attack you. What's the matter?'

She had to say something; he would not let it alone.

'Dake, I was married once, long ago. It...it ended suddenly. One day he just upped and left. I was devastated, hurt, bewildered. I don't ever want to suffer such pain again. Trips together...I don't know; I don't want complications. A purely business association I think I can manage, but nothing more. *Nothing*!' She drew a shaky breath, darted a quick look at him. 'Were you ever married?'

'No.'

The shaft hit home. It had been a farce, then. A sham. She felt suddenly wounded, bruised and heartsick; she had always thought it a genuine marriage. Her aunt had been right—what a fool Lani had been.

'Lani, I don't know what happened in your marriage, but he's gone, and things like that don't happen a second time. You are beautiful, refreshing, intelligent, and around others you seem to have a good sense of humour. I've not experienced it personally,' he said wryly. 'We are work colleagues and that relationship is important. I won't infringe on that. But I would like to get to know you better, have you know me. What do you think?'

His hands were warm on her shoulders, and slowly the fingers began to caress through the soft sweater, a friendly massage to ease tense muscles.

Her legs began to grow weak; it was all she could do to prevent herself from throwing her arms around him and drawing his head down for a kiss.

'Come on the trip. I promise to behave myself,' he said softly.

'But can I?' she said involuntarily.

His eyes lit up and his warm smile broke across his face. 'Maybe not, but then we'll both enjoy it.'

She blushed; she couldn't believe she'd said the words aloud.

Dake's expression faded; one of intense concentration replaced his smile as his eyes gazed into her silvery grey ones, then dropped to her lips. She licked them unconsciously and he moved towards her. She held her breath as he drew closer, stopping only inches away. She was conscious of the weight of his fingers on her shoulders, the warmth emanating from his body, the soft swirl of air as he breathed out. Suddenly he spun around and walked behind the sofa.

'If you're going on this trip, I think we should review the strategy I drafted so that we present a united front before the client.' His breathing was ragged; she could see he was fighting for control and it gave her strength. So he wasn't totally immune to her, either. Somehow that was comforting.

'I'll fix us some coffee; you get the plans out.'

She needed the breathing space to collect her thoughts, regroup and be able to present a serene demeanour before this distracting man.

When she returned, Dake had laid out the files, charts and spreadsheets he had brought. They covered her coffee-table. She pushed one file aside to put down the tray, then sat beside him, at a safe distance, and looked to him to set the tone.

'The way I see it, we need to build public opinion and that of the employees against the take-over. There are one or two long-range reasons why it won't be in the company's best interest, but they are speculative right now. I don't want the short-term gain to dazzle everyone.'

Lani marvelled that men could turn on and off their emotions so easily. He was all business. It was as if the last few moments had never occurred. If she wanted to compete in this man's world, she'd better at least pretend she could turn off her emotions as easily.

They reviewed each aspect of the plan until Dake was convinced they were on the same wavelength and could present a cohesive presentation to the senior management of the client. It was late when they finished, the coffee gone and the fire replenished numerous times.

Dake stretched, arms high, letting them fall to the back of the sofa. Lani gathered up their cups, put them on the tray. Now that they had concluded the review, would he leave? She glanced at her watch; it was after midnight.

'So, Lani, tell me a little about yourself,' he invited.

'Like what?' She leaned back. A mistake. His hand was only inches from her skin. She imagined she could feel the heat from it travelling the small distance to her neck and shoulder. She'd look silly moving, but she was dramatically aware of his proximity, his eyes penetrating in his observation, his shoulders wide and strong.

'You had a whole dossier on me from the interview. I met the others, talked about the job and a little about each of them. But you I missed, both times. How long have you been with the company? When did you get this place? Where are you from? What do you like to do when not at work?'

'I started with Sanderson's over eight years ago, almost at the bottom. I've worked hard, studying nights, getting help from others at the firm. It's paid off. I got this place last year, when I was promoted to director.'

She fell silent, staring at the fire. She didn't want to start this. When would he stop this cat and mouse game?

'Work history is OK, personal is not?'

She glanced up at him from under her lashes, her eyes silver in the firelight. He was astute. Her best bet with this man was to stay away, not let herself be drawn in by his charm again.

Yet he seemed genuinely interested, wanted to know more about her. Could she tell him of her past; would it be what he wanted, spark his memory? Or was he only toying with her? What if she confronted him, exposed her knowledge of who he was, of their previous relationship? What would his reaction be then? Would he have dozens of reasons for leaving her, for not contacting her all these years? Had he even wondered about her during the last ten years?

She was afraid to find out.

'My folks died when I was young. I was raised by my aunt. She died while I was in college.' Alone and estranged from her niece, another consequence of Dake's desertion.

'Was that when you were married?' he asked.

Her eyes filled with tears. It was when she had thought herself married. She said nothing, commanding herself to have enough control to keep the tears from falling.

'He must have been a bastard to have hurt you so much,' Dake said softly.

'I rather think he was,' she replied tightly, looking directly at him.

'I didn't mean to upset you by raking up old memories.'

'Raking them up or creating them, what's the difference?' she asked bitterly.

He moved closer, his hand dropping to caress the column of her neck, his fingers slipping beneath the edge of her collar.

'I want us to only have happy memories, never bad ones.'

Lani trembled, drowning in the depth of his brown eyes, lost in the endless ages of the promise his touch brought. Had he said those same words years ago?

His hand was warm and gentle as he caressed her, and she leaned back against it, closing her eyes to shut out all sensations except for the exquisiteness of his touch, the feathery caresses of his fingers against her skin, the sudden feeling of homecoming.

His fingers were warm but they sent chills of excitement and anticipation along Lani's skin. His touch was light, yet she felt it to her soul.

When he moved against the cushions, her eyes flew open. Fear and disgust warred within her. She shrank against the back of the sofa, unwilling to let him proceed.

'It's late,' she whispered. 'You'd better go.'

Disappointment flashed briefly in his eyes, but he slowly sat back and nodded.

'You're right. But fair warning, I'll come again.'

He packed his papers and stood, tall and dark, suddenly a stranger. Not the dashing young man of her youth. He was assured, confident, dynamic. Why was he toying with her? Wouldn't it be better to clear the air and go on? Yet she hesitated. Was he also hesitating to bring it up?

Lani rose and led the way to the door like an automaton. This evening had been a strain, in more than one way. But she felt a small sense of accomplishment. She'd made it through!

He paused at the door and looked down at her. 'A kiss for the road?'

'Between business colleagues?' she replied primly.

He smiled at her tone. 'Soon to become friends, I hope.'

He leaned over and lightly brushed her lips with his. 'See you at the airport on Monday. We have a nine a.m. flight to the coast.'

CHAPTER FOUR

LANI approached her flight with trepidation. She didn't want to make this trip, would give almost anything to get out of it, but she was trapped and she knew it. Putting on a bright, artificial smile, she headed towards the gate, feeling as a prisoner might, making the walk to gaol.

Lani saw Dake first. He was standing off to one side, towering over the others awaiting the plane. She was surprised to see Mark, too. Was he going? Her spirits lightened.

'Hi, Lani,' Mark called when he spotted her.

Dake turned slowly, a smile lighting his face as he watched Lani walk towards him. His glance was casual, running down the length of her, from her warm dark blue woollen overcoat, with its bright scarlet scarf, down to her trim navy pumps. The wool suit she wore beneath the coat was navy and the blouse white and blue. It was a conservative outfit that travelled well. Her hair was in a French plait, her make-up subtly applied. She was as ready as she'd ever be.

'Good morning,' Dake said.

'Hi. Mark, I didn't know you were going,' she said, smiling happily at him.

'Recruited at the last minute,' he grumbled good-naturedly. 'Dake thinks we need a strong financial showing so I'm dazzling them with spreadsheets. Now that you're here, I can leave Dake alone. He was worried you wouldn't show. I'm going for a paper; either of you want something?'

She shook her head, glancing at Dake. So he had been worried she wouldn't come after all. Interesting.

Dake smiled sardonically down at Lani as Mark walked away. 'You needn't look so pleased there's another traveller. Did you think we needed a chaperon?'

'Don't be silly,' she murmured, irritated that she was so transparent. She was relieved that Mark was going with them, but angry with herself for making it so blatantly obvious.

As the airline announced the flight, she smiled brightly.

'So they're on time?' she asked to make conversation, to make the trip normal. Her throat was tight with strain and tension. How would she ever make it to the west coast?

'Yes—at least something's going right,' Mark grumbled, a folded paper beneath his arm.

'What's the matter with you?'

'They don't have the latest edition of the *Herald*.'

'Come on, Mark, that's not enough to upset you. What's up?'

'Oh, the baby was up all last night. We didn't know what was wrong with him. Both Beth and I tried everything. He finally dropped off just as I was leaving. I called Beth a few minutes ago and he's still asleep. I'm dead on my feet.' Mark drew a weary hand across his eyes.

'I'm sure he'll be fine. I know you're tired, but think how glad Beth was that you were home. It would be worse for her if he were sick tonight.'

Lani remembered how panicked she had been the first time Annalise had been sick. She had had no one to turn to, no one to offer support, to help her care for the baby. She looked over at Dake, and away quickly. He should have been with her, supported her during Annalise's infancy. Where had he been then? She thought back to his resumé. He'd been working at a bank in Chicago.

'We have three seats together in the business class, so we can review the proposal, and the information we need from this meeting,' Dake said as they began boarding. Lani nodded in agreement, thankful for a business slant to the journey. *She had to stop remembering*. The past was gone, nothing could change it. She had to look forward, not back.

Mark sat by the window, Dake in the middle, and Lani took the aisle seat. As soon as they were airborne, Dake took his briefcase out and withdrew the folders concerning Forscue Industries. He turned towards Mark and the two reviewed the financial information they had received from the beleaguered company. Lani listened absently, her mind wandering as they went deeper into financial analysis.

Lani would miss her daughter, though Annalise would be fine staying with Mrs Palmer. Lani had been so lucky to find that lady. She had had Annalise in day-care since she was a baby. Most of the centres she'd tried were fine for parents where one or the other could drop off or pick up. The hours were limited, and there were no exceptions. If Lani had to work late, she had to pick up Annalise and then try to find a baby-sitter for the evening at short notice before returning to work. It had not been easy.

A lot of her life since her husband had left had not been easy. A baby-sitter, finding a place they could afford where she felt safe, and basics like food and clothes, all had been hard to come by. But she had never given up, never failed in her efforts to be the best mother to Annalise that she could.

When they moved into the apartment last year, Nora Harrington had recommended Mrs Palmer. It had been love at first sight. The woman loved children, had six of her own and now took in a few children, to keep her hand in, as she said. She'd taken Annalise, and Lani had at last found a woman who would watch her child until she came for her, even on overnight trips.

That worry taken care of, the only one left occupying Lani's thoughts was Dake Morgan. She ought to talk to him, confront him, find out why he'd left, and why he was now acting as if he didn't know her from Adam. She ought to, but not just yet.

She shook her head. Time enough to face that when and if it came. The nagging feeling that she should confront him had plagued her all weekend, but she was reluctant to do so. One day, maybe. She didn't like the idea, but she had to admit she was afraid to hear exactly what he would say.

If he didn't bring it up, did that mean he wanted to ignore their past? Then why the kiss on Friday?

She pulled her own folders from her briefcase and reviewed the plan she'd gone over with John last week and Dake last Friday, noting in the margins the dates she had scheduled over the weekend.

After the meal had been cleared away Dake turned to Lani. 'We went over your material on Friday; is there anything else we should cover?'

'Only the schedule of news releases.' She drew the folder out and spread the schedule she had drafted yesterday. Dake studied the plan, checking a couple of dates against notes he had, nodding as he returned the sheet.

'Looks good. I guess we're as ready as we're going to be.'

Lani studied Dake from beneath her lashes, curious as to what he had been doing these last few years, interested in learning more about him, how he'd matured and developed. Underneath all the external trappings of a trim body and good clothes, she still felt the pull of all that had attracted her to him in the first place: his sense of humour, his strength, his intelligence and his kindness.

But not to her. Or had that been his idea of kindness: a quick and final ending, no long-drawn-out goodbyes, no long rehashing of things gone wrong, just end it swiftly, completely? She had deserved an explanation, at least.

He turned his head slightly, saw her watching him, and gave her a slow, knowing smile. His gaze dropped to her mouth and she felt it like a jolt, remembering his brief kiss on Friday night.

'Know me again?' he asked softly.

She looked away. 'Sorry, I didn't mean to stare. I . . . I think that about covers it all. We should prove to them that we know what we're doing and that our plans will work.'

'I think so, I sure hope so. Excuse me a minute, I'll be back.'

Lani moved her legs aside so that he could leave his seat. Once he started towards the back, Mark glanced over at Lani.

'I'm dead tired. I won't be any good for anyone tomorrow if I don't get some rest. Wake me before we land, will you?'

'Sure, but it's only a couple of hours more.'

'I know, but it'll help. Then I can get to bed early tonight. I'll be fine tomorrow if I can just get some sleep!' Mark smiled tiredly and pulled the shades by his window. Stretching out as much as the crowded space permitted, he soon dropped off.

Lani moved to the middle seat, to make it easier for Dake when he returned. The seat was still warm from his body. She shifted slightly, feeling the warmth. Unbidden thoughts arose. Firmly refusing to dwell on the sensations those thoughts caused, she moved again to get comfortable, her head dropping back against the seat-rest.

The trip wasn't proving to be the problem she'd feared. Mark's being along helped. Maybe it would be an ordinary business trip after all. She'd gone on them with Peter. But then she'd never felt for Peter what she felt for Dake.

Which was what, exactly? she asked herself.

'Playing musical chairs?' Dake's warm voice sounded in her ear.

Lani opened her eyes and smiled at him. 'Mark's going to sleep. Thought I'd just make it easier for you when you came back. Did you want this one?'

'No, the aisle is fine. If we're finished planning for Forscue, how about that interview you so adroitly avoid every time I bring it up?'

'Now why should I avoid an interview? You're the one being interviewed,' Lani pointed out.

'Good question, one I've repeatedly asked myself. Yet I think of an interview as a two-way street; you find out about me, I find out about you.'

'Isn't it too late? You already have the job.'

'But I don't know about you, the unknown executive.'

She smiled shyly, nervously. Still unknown, or was he only pretending lack of recognition? What would jog his memory, or provoke a revelation?

'You ask me a question. After I answer, I'll ask you one,' he suggested, devilish lights dancing in his brown eyes.

Lani bit her lip, seeing the trap. She didn't want to reveal anything to this man. It was a strain just dealing with him in business. How would she fare if they got personal? She cast around for an innocuous question.

'OK, where are you from?'

Dake's smile faded, and he looked strained, embarrassed. 'Chicago,' he said briefly.

Lani frowned. He'd been born in New York. Did he think she meant his last place?

'Where are you from, Lani?' he asked.

'Ingram, a small place just outside Pittsburgh. It's nice, as small towns go. As I said, my aunt Polly raised me. We had a good life.' She had died when Lani was in college. She still missed her. 'She was my only family.'

'I have no family.'

Of course; it had been one of the things that had drawn them together. Together they would create their own family. Or so she had thought. Together they were to do a lot of things. Only together had ended abruptly one April day ten years ago.

Lani remembered Dake talking about his mother, how much he had loved her, how he had missed her. Her name had been Annalise. Lani had named their daughter after her, wanting her daughter to have something from her father's side.

His father had been different—driving, forceful, always out for more money, more status, more power. Ruthless in his goals, not above manipulating people and circumstances for his own purposes, so Dake had said. He had not missed his father.

Talking about her aunt brought it all back. How she'd loved Aunt Polly, the rift between them when her aunt had found out about the baby, the awful blackness that had come over Lani when her aunt died. She shook off the depression, trying to remember some of the things Dake had told her when they had been living together.

He hadn't talked much about his family, yet at the time she'd been so wrapped up in the two of them that she hadn't given it much thought. Now it explained why he could walk away from her without a backward glance. He had learned to be hard and ruthless from his father.

She closed her eyes, thinking back to the happy days they'd shared and all the promise she thought their marriage held. The familiar ache began again when she thought of his walking out with no word. Never calling, never writing. She'd been frantic. Was he safe, was he all right? That had changed to anger. How could he have deserted her? Then the awful realisation and resignation to how things were.

A tear trickled down her cheek. When a warm finger brushed it away, her eyes flew open to gaze into Dake's concerned ones.

'What's this?' he asked, holding up his finger with the tear glistening.

Giving a shaky smile, she replied, 'Nothing, just old, sad memories.'

His mouth tightened. 'Don't shut me out, Lani. I want to be your friend.'

As you were before?

She was afraid to speak for fear of what she'd say.

His hand reached out to cover hers, his fingers warm and comforting. She gently withdrew her hand. His touch was too disturbing.

Just being beside him brought feelings long forgotten to the surface. She closed her eyes, feigning sleep. If he'd leave her alone, she could maintain her control. Resist throwing herself into his arms, demanding he kiss her, hold her, love her. Turn back the clock to a happier time.

But how she wished she could!

CHAPTER FIVE

THE ride to Calavaras County, home of Forscue Industries, took over three hours. It passed faster than Lani had expected because of Mark. While Dake drove, Mark directed. Lani sat in the back, angled so that she could watch Dake as he drove, yet he could not see her in the rear-view mirror. She was content to let it be so. She studied how he'd changed, matured. He had not lacked self-confidence before, but now he evidenced even more, with just a trace of arrogance.

His hair was still thick, wavy, dark. Her fingers tingled with desire to touch it, feel its texture, its thickness. His shoulders were broad, his hands large, capable, strong. His expensive clothes fitted him well. He was a sexy, handsome man.

Dake and Mark discussed the coming presentation, the scenery they were passing, and the fact that they were both avid skiers. Lani listened half-heartedly, trying to rationalise the discovery she'd just made. She still wanted this man!

She had been so in love with him years ago. She wasn't in love with him now, but she wanted him. Wanted him to pay attention to her, wanted him to be with her, wanted him to want her in all the ways a man wanted a woman. She pushed the thoughts from her mind—too dangerous. Their relationship was strictly business. She would not put her heart in jeopardy a second time. She would not give in to the longing which arose. Once burned was enough for anyone.

He had been at Sanderson's for two weeks and still hadn't said a word about their past. No innuendoes, no knowing looks, nothing. Why? She puzzled through it. Was there any advantage in not bringing up the past? Only if he was afraid of a scene.

But she wouldn't do that. She, too, had matured over the years. Experience was sometimes a harsh teacher, but she could cope with a discussion.

Why not bring it up herself? She shied away from the idea. Wryly she admitted that she wasn't ready. She didn't want it brought up. Not just yet. Especially not on a business trip.

The first meeting with Forscue was set for nine in the morning. It was just approaching the dinner hour when they checked into the old hotel near the centre of town. Calavaras City was an old gold town which had kept pace with its citizens and made the move into the twentieth century. While it was a small town when compared to Boston, there were several national chains, from the local Safeway, to a McDonald's, to the Ramada Inn.

Lani excused herself from the two men when they checked in.

'I'm tired, and want to get a good night's rest before the show tomorrow,' she explained, pointing out her bags to the porter.

'We'll meet for breakfast at seven, in the dining-room. Our meeting is set for nine a.m. and I want to be prompt,' Dake said.

'I'll be here. Goodnight.'

'Goodnight, Lani,' Mark muttered. 'Dake, I'm for an early evening myself. Need anything before I get my room?'

Lani didn't hear Dake's response. She reached the lifts, and was soon in her room.

She called Annalise to let her know she'd arrived safely, and to hear how her day had gone. Talking to her daughter brightened her spirits, and for the first time Lani thought of Annalise's father with pity. She was sorry he couldn't see Annalise grow up. Sorry for all he'd missed. Dake would make a great father. A child would feel safe and secure around him. He would teach it good from bad, right from wrong. Lani paused. How would he explain leaving her the way he had?

It was late when Lani prepared for bed. She had brought a mystery to read, and been so engrossed in it that she lost track of the time. Disgusted with herself, she rushed to prepare for bed. She had wanted a good night's rest in preparation for the morning's presentation.

The tap on the door was faint. Lani cocked her head. Had she heard a knock? It sounded again, on the connecting door.

Lani stood still, her robe half on, half off. She shrugged it back on, and moved slowly towards the door. Dake had the adjacent room. Mark's was the one beyond. Did Dake think it all right to use the connecting door as a convenience?

If he thought that, she had something to say about it.

When the tap came again, she stormed to the door and snatched at the lock. She'd set him straight, in no uncertain terms!

Flinging open the door, she was startled into silence by the sight before her.

Dake leaned shakily against the door-jamb, one hand cradling the other, wrapped in a towel. His shirt was unbuttoned, exposing a healthy expanse of tanned chest.

Sheepishly, Dake grinned at her. 'Sorry, but I've had an accident and need some help. You were closer than Mark, because of the connecting door. But I didn't know if you were still awake or not.'

His eyes ran swiftly over her, noting with appreciation the pale peach lace and beribboned nightie with matching robe.

'What happened?' She stared at the wrapped hand.

'I broke a travelling mirror. When I tried to pick up the pieces, I stupidly cut a couple of fingers. On my right hand, of course. I can't seem to get the bleeding to stop. Do you have a first-aid kit? Some bandages?'

'Yes, go on into the bathroom, I'll be right there.'

Lani backed into her room and ran to her suitcase to fetch the first-aid kit she always carried. It was a habit from the holidays she and

Annalise took. Glad she had it, she hurried into the bathroom.

Dake stood by the sink, gingerly unwrapping the towel. As he did so, more and more of it was exposed, bright red with blood. His first two fingers were heavily bleeding. He'd sliced them deep, right across the fleshy part.

'Your fingerprints will never be the same,' she said, idiotically, distressed at the amount of blood. 'Can you stand to let me run some cool water on them?' she asked, turning the tap on gently and taking his hand. A quick glance at his face and she knew he was in considerable pain. 'It'll sting,' she said, sympathetically.

He gritted his teeth and nodded, his eyes on the blood welling up and dripping on the pristine sink. Perspiration beaded his forehead, his upper lip.

Lani felt a tug of compassion, hating to hurt him, but wanting to wash some of the blood away so that she could see the cuts.

Gently she drew his hand beneath the water's trickle. She heard his sharp intake of breath as the water stung the wounds. She felt his distress as if it were her own. Her hands trembled, holding his. Wanting to stop, to run from the scene, she stood firm, determined to do the right thing. If only she could be as dispassionate as a nurse, not think of whose hand she held, of the pain he was enduring.

The blood continued to well up as fast as she could wash it away. Lani became concerned.

'I think you need stitches, Dake. The cuts look awfully deep and the bleeding just won't stop.'

'Damn fool thing to do,' he muttered, pulling his hand away. The fingers were immediately covered with blood.

'Here.' She took one of her clean towels and pressed it against his fingers, trying to staunch the flow. 'Come in and lie down. I'll call for the hotel doctor.'

She led him into the bedroom, to her bed. Easing him down, she noted how pale he looked. Gratefully he sank on the bed, lay back against the pillows, his injured hand held by his good one.

Lani dialled Reception. As she talked, she watched him, trying to assess if he was paler than usual. With his eyes closed, his mouth drawn in pain, he looked younger, more defenceless, vulnerable. Lani hated him being in such pain. She wanted to soothe him, make the pain go away.

She replaced the receiver and moved to sit beside him on the bed.

'He'll be here as soon as they can locate him. Are you all right?' she asked. Her fingers ached to brush back the lock of hair that had fallen out of place, to pat his shoulders, soothe away the pain. But she held herself rigid.

'I'll live, if that's what you want to know. Damn, you wouldn't think a little cut could hurt so much.'

'I don't think they're so little; they seem pretty deep. You look as if you've lost a lot of blood.'

'Fingers always bleed a lot,' he murmured, closing his eyes again.

'I thought that was head wounds,' she replied, more to distract him.

As the minutes ticked by, Lani became aware of the proximity of the two of them, of the tanned wall of his chest, tapering to a flat stomach, the hard nubs of his nipples, the muscles criss-crossing his ribs. Resolutely she kept her eyes away from the tantalising expanse of warm skin exposed by the open flaps of his shirt.

But it wasn't easy. Her hands yearned to trace his muscles, to feel his warmth beneath them. Her eyes moved upwards, to his lips, held in a tight line. They'd been soft and wonderful when he'd kissed her last Friday. Would he kiss her again? Did she want him to? Would his kisses be as erotic as they had been years ago? Was he even more accomplished now?

Lani jumped up from the bed and moved away.

'What is it?' Dake opened his eyes.

'I . . . I thought I heard the doctor.' She moved to the door and opened it. The hallway was empty. Slowly closing the door, she turned back to him.

'Are you warm enough?' she asked. 'People in shock need to be kept warm.'

'It is a little chilly. But I'll be fine.'

'Sit up and I'll cover you.' She reached around him to pull the covers down, leaning over him, her arm brushing against his shoulder as she pulled the blanket and sheet away from the pillows.

'Can you stand for just a sec?'

He leaned forward and stood, Lani's arm holding his waist, her other yanking down the blanket.

'There, lie back.' She drew the blanket over him, tucking it around his shoulders, using the action to let her fingers linger just a moment longer than they needed, feeling the warmth of his body, the strength of his muscles. Chancing a glance at him, she saw the twinkle in his eyes. Blushing, she stepped back, confused.

'Thanks, Mama,' he said, chuckling softly at her confusion.

The knock on the door saved Lani from replying.

The hotel doctor quickly the assessed the situation and ushered Dake into the bathroom, to use it as a surgery. Giving Dake a pain-killer, he then proceeded to place four neat stitches in each finger. Lani served as nurse, and was relieved to see the bleeding finally stop.

'Get right back into bed, young man,' the doctor said as he packed his bag. 'Don't get those fingers wet for a week. Your lovely wife will just have to help you in the shower,' he said jovially, giving Lani a wink.

She blushed beet-red, refusing to look at Dake, refusing to even think of what the doctor suggested. She calmly saw him to the door and turned to find Dake struggling to keep from laughing. His eyes danced with amusement and when he saw Lani's outraged expression he gave up and burst out laughing.

'Oh, your face—it was priceless. The staid and stand-offish Ms Williams told to help me in the shower!'

She was instantly hurt. Was that how he saw her, as staid and stand-offish?

'I'm sure you can manage just fine,' she said coldly.

He nodded, his smile fading. 'Except for shaving. If I need help with that, will you?'

'Ask Mark. Do you need anything else before you get to bed?' she asked, standing by the connecting door. She wanted him to leave!

He hesitated a moment. 'It's hard to use these fingers; they're very sore. Would you mind unfastening the top of my trousers? I won't need help with pyjamas; I sleep in the nude.'

She stared at him, the heat invading her body. It was a reasonable request. Why wake Mark just for that? But she wasn't sure she could do it. Slowly she stepped across the room to him. It couldn't take more than three seconds. Pretend he was a stranger.

She didn't unfasten the top of strangers' trousers. She took a deep breath and reached out. The material was snug across his waist. She tried to unfasten it without touching him. It was impossible. Determined to do it, and not give rise to any remarks on his part, she slid her fingers behind the waistband. His skin was hot, taut, disturbing. She grasped the material, tried to force the button through the hole, but couldn't. She felt all thumbs. Intensely aware of him, of where her hands were, of what they had been to each other, she could scarcely concentrate. The picture of Dake sleeping in the nude was all she could see.

He stood still, arms at his side, patiently waiting. When she was at last successful, he let his breath out in a gasp.

'Thanks for helping me, Lani; you weren't stand-offish tonight.'

'I...' Before she could say anything, his mouth closed on hers, blocking all conscious thought. Lani savoured the feel of his lips as they gently moved against hers. It was too fleeting.

When he drew back, she managed to squeak out, 'You're welcome. Leave the door open; if you need anything in the night, just call.'

Watching as he moved into his room, Lani felt as if the world had shifted again. Was she falling in love again?

When Lani awoke the next morning, the connecting door was closed. She moved to it, leaning her ear against it, trying to hear if he was up and moving about. Satisfied when she heard noises on his side, she began to get dressed.

Entering the dining-room promptly at seven, Lani saw Mark and Dake seated at a table near the window, coffee before them.

'Good morning. How are you feeling, Dake?' She joined them, pleased to note they had a cup waiting for her.

'Better, thanks. I was telling Mark about our escapade. Lani would make a fine mother,' Dake said, smiling at her.

Joel had not told him, then.

She smiled perfunctorily and looked sharply at Mark. He closed his mouth, obviously having second thoughts about what he was about to say. Lani firmly changed the subject.

The presentation at Forscue went as planned, the three of them working well together, as if they had been together for years. They were able to respond to all questions Forscue management posed, anticipating some questions, providing new ideas to the company. They reviewed the strategic plan, and time schedule. The Forscue staff were pleased with the programme as outlined.

Lani spent the afternoon interviewing dozens of people, from supervisors to general plant personnel. She made arrangements to receive copies of the employee newsletter and the most recent press releases the company had issued. Even as she listened, she began formulating the communications she knew would be most effective.

Wednesday saw them travelling to the first of two branch offices, the one near Lake Tahoe. Thursday they visited the second, on the coast near Fort Bragg.

Friday they flew home. There had been no more tête-à-têtes between Lani and Dake. It had been purely business from Tuesday's breakfast on. She was relieved she didn't have to contend with anything distracting. She needed to devote her energies to the work at hand.

As she sank into the window-seat on the plane from San Francisco, Lani reviewed the visit. She was satisfied. It had gone pretty much as all the ones with Peter had. She was a professional and worked as one. Dake would have no reason to find fault with her performance.

She wanted him to appreciate what she could do, how far she'd come from the naïve little student he had known. Maybe show him what he had missed.

He sat beside her, Mark on the aisle. As they taxied out on the runway, Dake turned to Lani. 'I liked the way you handled that plant manager yesterday. Do you find it a problem, being the only woman on some of these projects?'

'No, I don't find too many chauvinistic remarks like yesterday's. I've learned to deal with those I do get.'

'It's not something men think about too often.'

'Most men think women should get married and stay home.'

'Is that so bad?' Dake asked.

'I don't think it's bad, but it isn't an option available to every woman.'

Dake studied her for a long moment before looking away. At least he offered no platitudes.

Lani's luggage was among the first on the carousel. Anxious to get Annalise and head for home, she gave a quick wave to her travelling companions and left. She picked up Annalise and Judith-Ann, who was staying the night. She was glad to be home, to have her daughter with her. Even Judith-Ann's spending the night was fine, normal, routine.

Lani needed a breathing space. She was becoming obsessed with thoughts of Dake Morgan. She'd spend the evening with the girls, and push all thoughts of Dake Morgan from her mind.

'Pizza, right?' she asked as they entered their home.

'Yes, with everything, right, Judith-Ann?' Annalise exclaimed. 'Get a large, Mama, so we can have left-overs tomorrow.'

'OK. I'll change, and after we eat we'll make brownies. You girls can get the ingredients out.'

'Oh, boy, this is going to be fun, Annalise,' Judith-Ann said. She was always willing to fall in with whatever Annalise wanted to do.

Lani hastily unpacked, hanging up her suits, putting away her suitcase. She changed into jeans and a warm pink sweater, brushing out her hair and washing off all make-up. It was good to be home, to relax. She wouldn't even think of work until Monday morning!

As Lani descended the stairs she heard a knock at the door. The stampede of feet let her know that Annalise and Judith-Ann were taking care of it. The pizza service was improving.

She stopped dead in her tracks when she heard the familiar voice.

'Hi, I'm looking for Lani Williams.' It was Dake.

'*Mom*!' Annalise yelled, not moving from the front door. 'Someone here to see you.'

Wishing the floor could open up and swallow her, Lani forced herself to move forward. Dake's

face wore a look of astonishment, clearing when
he saw Lani. He smiled as he took in the loose
hair swirling around her shoulders, the fresh,
scrubbed look to her face.

'Hi.'

'Hi.' She was tongue-tied. Annalise and Judith-
Ann were silent, both staring solemnly at the two
adults.

'You dashed from the airport so fast I didn't
get a chance to see if you wanted to have dinner
with me tonight.'

Lani noticed he'd changed as well. His dark
cords fitted him like a second skin, and his navy
pullover was pushed up over tanned arms. She
swallowed hard as the seconds ticked by.

'We've ordered dinner,' she said at last.

'It's pizza,' Judith-Ann added.

'But we've got lots. Why don't you ask your
friend to stay to supper, Mama?' Annalise said
in a voice suddenly reminiscent of Lani's own.

'I'd like that.' Dake's eyes never left Lani's
face. He stood in the open doorway, watching
her.

'Yes, do, if you'd really want to.'

'We're making brownies, later, after we eat.
You can help if you like,' Annalise offered
generously.

'I would love to. Home-made brownies are my
favourite.'

The girls ran upstairs to Annalise's room,
taking Judith-Ann's suitcase as Dake closed the
door. He smiled easily at Lani.

'You look about twenty tonight. Are you really the mother to that young lady?'

Lani nodded. What would he say if she introduced Annalise as his daughter?

CHAPTER SIX

'Is IT all right with you if I stay?' Dake asked.

'I guess so; you caught me by surprise. I didn't get a chance to introduce you to my daughter and her friend. I'll remedy that as soon as they come down.'

Lani felt awkward; she didn't want him to stay, to invade her life, imprint himself on all aspects. Yet how could she refuse? One part of her clamoured for his attention; the more prudent part warned her away.

'I didn't know you had a daughter.'

'Oh? Well, I do.' She pretended surprise that he didn't know, though she herself had tried to keep him from finding out. 'The pizza should be here soon.'

He raised his left hand to gently finger the shiny tresses of her light brown hair swirling around her shoulders.

'It's so pretty, you should always let it go unconfined.'

'Hardly a professional look,' she said drily, her knees weak, the blood pounding in her ears.

'But pretty,' he said softly, his eyes drawn to her lips. His fingers were gentle against her shoulder, moving to the back of her neck as he drew her closer.

The kiss was warm and unexpected. Lani had no chance to respond or pull away. Before she realised what was happening, it was over. His eyes gazed down into hers as the two girls noisily erupted down the stairs.

'The pizza's here, it's here, Mom!' Annalise dashed by and flung open the door, she and Judith-Ann dancing with impatience by the door.

Lani stepped back, glad of the interruption. She was having trouble remembering her resolution to have nothing to do with him.

Between the four of them they made short work of the pizza. The girls accepted Dake as if he'd been coming around for years. Lani relaxed once she'd mentioned her daughter's name. Dake smiled and said it was a pretty name. That hurdle safely passed, Lani somehow knew she had no need to worry about a confrontation tonight. Yet would she ever be free of the weight of the past? Would it be better to get it over with?

Once the pizza was devoured, they all moved to the kitchen to begin baking brownies. With each of them wanting a different variation, they solved the decision-making process by agreeing to make four different batches.

'Though everyone has to take some home,' she said, looking pointedly at Dake.

'No problem with me. I love brownies.'

'Me too,' Judith-Ann piped up.

As they mixed the batches and poured them into pans, amid jokes, and laughter, an odd ache took Lani by surprise. She was happy, happier than she'd been in a long time. She wished she could capture this night to hold and re-live whenever she wanted. The picture of Dake leaning close to Annalise she committed to memory. If he had stayed they might have had many such happy memories.

She was reminded also of her own childhood. She remembered her aunt Polly spending hours in the kitchen with Lani when she'd been younger, making goodies to eat and share with neighbours. They'd had such fun times, all of which had cost them very little, since they had had so little. But Polly had given of herself and found activities that emphasised their love and the bond between them, not something that cost money.

Dake glanced up and caught her eye.

'This is fun, Lani. I don't remember helping as a kid.'

'Is that why you hold that spoon so awkwardly? And I thought it was because of the bandages on your fingers.' Lani smiled back. He was stirring a thick batch, using only two fingers of his right hand to hold the spoon.

'I do know how to cook, you know,' he said loftily, handing her the bowl and spoon. 'But I'm injured and need to be pampered, not driven.'

'What are you contributing to this project, then, may I ask?' she teased.

'I shall bring the biggest appetite. Once the brownies are done, I'll be the official taster.'

'I want to be,' Annalise said.

'Me too,' Judith-Ann said.

'We can all be,' Dake announced diplomatically.

When the first batch was out of the oven, the girls were given a big piece each and sent to watch the movie that was just starting. Another batch was placed in the oven and Lani started filling the last pan when she sighed.

'Problem?' Dake asked, watching her work.

'Just look at this kitchen. I think most of the tasters have forgotten there is still clean-up.'

'I'll do it.'

'Not with those fingers that can't get wet. I'll just put everything in soak and do them in the morning. I'm tired now, and just want to sit down and rest. It's been a long day.'

She scraped the sides of the bowl, wiping the last little bit from the spatula with her fingers. Setting the empty bowl in the sink, she ran water in it.

Before she could wash her hand, however, Dake moved beside her and took her hand in his. Slowly, watching her with deep, dark, fathomless eyes, he raised her hand to his lips. In turn, he caressed each fingertip, gently licking the chocolate batter, his lips a wild delight, the tantalising feel of his tongue against her skin an unexpected sensation of sensuous tactile feeling. She felt the shock of his touch to the centre of her being.

Lani felt drawn into his gaze, as if she was drowning in pure emotion. Each finger was kissed, taken into his mouth, cleansed by the gentle erotic touch of his tongue, released as he moved to the next finger. His eyes held hers, dark and smouldering.

Lani began to tremble, her heart pounding so strongly she imagined he must see it beneath her sweater. Her knees were weak, her breath came in short bursts. She felt incredibly weak, cherished, desired.

'Dake...'

He was virile, sexy, exciting. Was she remembering the past, or was she drawn to Dake *today*? She wanted to lock them in an empty room and talk and kiss and make love. Was she falling in love with Dake Morgan?

He released her hand and drew her into his arms, his mouth descending on hers. His lips were warm and he tasted of brownies. She relaxed against him, delighting in the strength of his body, the ardour of his passion. His arms drew her unresistingly against him as he moulded her to his body. His left hand gently rubbed her back, moving her closer and closer. She could feel the strong muscles of his legs, the firm wall of his chest. His arms displayed warm strength, his hands gently brought her closer, even closer...

Lani lost conscious thought of everything but his lips and mouth, his body against hers. Was she floating, dreaming, flying? He moved against her, opening her mouth slightly to taste the sweet delights within. His tongue gently traced her inner lips, building the fire, then moved to plunder the softness, the moistness, to bring pleasure beyond all she'd experienced before in a kiss.

The oven buzzer sounded, ending the magical moment.

Lani drew back, dazed. She moved away, automatically reaching for the oven mitt, removing the brownies, placing the new pan on the oven shelf, taking her time, to collect herself, before she faced him again. She needed to let Dake know how she felt about what he'd done, how she felt about the present.

She felt guilty, knowing who he was, knowing he'd deserted her before, and yet still she was drawn by his power to excite, entice, entrap. She'd have to face it, confront him, and get the past resolved before she could ever be free for the present. She knew she could not trust him. Was any relationship possible without trust? They needed to talk. Maybe tonight, after Annalise was asleep.

She heard the sound of cutlery and turned to see Dake stacking pans and bowls in the sink, running the water, careful to hold his injured fingers clear.

'I'll do those; take these in to the girls. I'll be in as soon as I get these rinsed. You can watch the movie with them.' She thrust the plate of brownies at him, anxious for him to be gone. She wanted some time to herself.

'Are you going to be long?'

'No, I'll fix some coffee, too.'

Lani argued with herself as she quickly did the bowls and pans. She ought to tell him tonight that she didn't want to see him again. She ought to, but still she hesitated. She didn't trust him; she didn't trust herself.

Lani waited for the coffee, her mind in turmoil. She bit her lip in indecision. Should she bring it up? Why hadn't he? Maybe she'd wait a little longer. If he was going to be in Boston permanently, she'd have to face it some time, talk to him some time. It didn't have to be tonight.

When she joined them a few minutes later, it seemed as if Dake and Annalise were getting along fine. She was sitting beside him on the sofa, and they were laughing together over something. The TV was playing a commercial and they had taken the time to talk. Gently putting down the coffee-tray, Lani sat on the other side of her daughter. It seemed safer.

That Dake thought the same thing was evident by his raised eyebrow and knowing grin. Lani ignored him and poured coffee.

'Mama, Dake has invited all of us to go to the beach on Sunday, even Judith-Ann. Can we go? Wouldn't it be fun, especially in winter? I've never been in winter. Besides, next weekend you're busy on Saturday; this weekend would be better.'

'Oh, honey, I don't know.' She looked up into Dake's intense gaze. His brown eyes were challenging, his face impassive. Dared she get involved?

'Not this weekend; I'm sure you're busy,' he said mockingly.

'Well...'

'I'll pick you up at eleven.'

Lani's mind went blank. Couldn't she find something to do on Sunday?

'Oh, do say yes, Mama. Sunday would be super fun to go to the beach.'

'All right, Dake, Sunday.' With effort she broke eye contact and smiled at Annalise. 'Sunday we'll try it, if it's not raining. Judith-Ann will have to ask her mother, too.'

'So, what are you doing next Saturday?' Dake asked softly when the show had resumed and the two girls flung themselves on the rug before the TV.

'I'm going to the Sorenson charity ball. Haven't you received your invitation? I thought it was mandatory for all of the senior management of the firm.'

'I did see it, didn't pay much attention. A command performance?'

'Sort of, from John's point of view. I think it's a kind of thank-you from Sorenson's for all our efforts. Black tie, very formal, the event of the season here in Boston.'

'Do you already have an escort?'

She flushed slightly. She really didn't want to go, had planned on driving herself, so that, after making sure everyone from work saw her there, she could leave.

'I'm going by myself.'

'I could easily pick you up.'

'No...no, thank you anyway. I'll keep on with my plans. Did you have enough brownies?'

'Plenty, and don't change the subject. Why would a lovely woman like you prefer to go alone, especially when a stranger to town needs someone to go with?'

'Ask someone from work.'

'I am, but I can't get her to say yes.'

Lani smiled at this, but shook her head. 'I'll see you there, but I prefer to go by myself.'

'Not starting any rumours at work?' he suggested, pursuing the issue.

'Not staying any longer than I have to,' she shot back, then blushed, embarrassed that he'd found out her intent.

He leaned back and laughed. 'At least you're honest. And you can count on seeing me there.' The warmth in his eyes was disturbing. Lani turned to watch the movie, afraid to continue this conversation.

Dake left when the movie was over, his goodbye friendly. He took her hard warmly, then kissed the back of it lightly.

'If Annalise and Judith-Ann were in bed where they belong, I'd say goodnight differently,' he murmured for her ears alone.

She smiled shyly and tugged her hand free. 'Goodnight, Dake.'

Once the girls were settled for the night, Lani wandered back downstairs, quickly tidying the living-room, rinsing out the coffee-cups, putting away the bowls and pans.

There was one thing more she wanted to do before going to bed; she had thought about it constantly since the plane-ride west. She went to her desk and sat down. Opening the bottom drawer, she withdrew a metal file box, setting it

carefully on her desk. It was her secret box. When
Annalise had first seen it years ago, Lani had explained it was her special secret box, and Annalise
was not to go into it.

Opening the box, Lani sat silently for a long
moment, memories flooding through her. She
reached in and picked up the small stack of
photos. They had had such a short time together;
there weren't many pictures.

She flipped through them, looking at her
younger self, and the heart-stoppingly handsome
young man. It was a younger Dake, dashing,
devil-may-care, and seemingly in love. It was
strange looking at the pictures, knowing the man
had not stayed, had disappeared one day only to
turn up ten years later. The love they had shared
was shining through all the photos. Lani couldn't
help but smile, though her heart ached for the
bright promise they'd thought life held.

She laid them aside and drew out the papers.
Riffling through them, she came to the one she
wanted. Unfolding it carefully, she read the marriage licence carefully. The groom's name was
clearly written: Dake Joseph Morgan. The bride's
was slightly shaky: Melanie Patricia Williams.
She remembered how nervous and excited she had
been at the licensing bureau in the small Vermont
town. She had had no indication or premonition
of what the future held that day. She'd only been
deliriously happy.

Sighing gently for a life that had never materi-
alised, she put everything back and replaced the
box. The reason for his disappearance was still

unknown. Would she ever know? Only if she confronted him. She no longer believed he would bring it up. He did not seem to feel guilt or remorse. Did she really want to know?

CHAPTER SEVEN

LANI awoke early Sunday, not getting up, snuggling down in the warm covers, a vague feeling of impending doom pervading. She didn't want to go to the beach, didn't want to be drawn into a deepening interaction with Dake just yet. It would be safer, far more prudent, to keep her distance from him.

She dressed in jeans and a sweatshirt, pulling her hair back into a pony-tail. Making coffee for breakfast, she checked the time. Not too early to call and cancel. But the line was engaged. Impatient to get the call over, she tried again. Still engaged.

Lani ate toast and coffee absently, again trying the phone: engaged. She speculated as to whom Dake would be talking to for so long.

Annalise awoke full of high spirits for the day ahead. Lani tried to think of other activities which would be a satisfactory substitute when the proposed beach outing was cancelled, but she didn't think any of them would be as appealing to the girls as an autumn day at the shore.

Still, they could go to the Commons, play frisbee, walk the Freedom Trail; they'd not done that in a while.

She tried the phone again: still engaged.

Lani's nerves fluttered as eleven o'clock approached. Judith-Ann arrived, sharing the excitement Annalise evidenced, the novelty of a day at the beach in late autumn enough for high enthusiasm.

Lani tried Dake's place again from the kitchen phone. The engaged signal buzzed in her ear as the doorbell rang. Annalise and Judith-Ann ran to open it. She hung up and moved into the living-room, startled into stillness by Dake's presence.

He looked rugged and ready for adventure in stout hiking boots, faded jeans and a thick brown turtleneck sweater beneath a sheepskin jacket. He grinned at her over the heads of the excited children.

'I'm early,' he said.

'I tried to call you.' She slowly moved forward. 'But your line was busy.'

His grin spread. 'I thought you might have second thoughts, want to cancel, so I took the phone off the hook last night. No changing your mind now; you wouldn't want to disappoint these two, would you?'

Lani looked down at the two girls, their exuberance dimmed as they listened to the exchange.

Resentfully she looked up into his dark eyes, the hint of triumph lurking.

'OK, we'll go,' she said resignedly.

'Dress warmly. I've got all the food and blankets in the car.'

A day at the beach could be fun, Lani thought hesitantly as she gathered her parka. With the girls there, how much could happen? Shrugging off her feelings of disquiet, she resolved to enjoy herself.

'I'm ready. Thanks for taking us,' she said politely, a smile lighting her face.

Dake's car was unexpected: a battered, dirty jeep. Lani stopped in surprise when she saw it; she had pictured him with a BMW or Mercedes.

'Like it?' he teased, noting her reaction.

'It's unexpected,' she murmured.

'It's super,' Annalise said enthusiastically.

The two girls happily scrambled into the back, Lani gingerly sat in the front. It was not the comfortable, luxurious vehicle she imagined he would own.

'Why a jeep?' she asked as he climbed in and turned the key.

'Gets me where I want to go, on or off the road. I leave status symbols to others.'

Lani lapsed into silence as they started. She watched the scenery passing on Commonwealth Avenue. Dake picked up Interstate-93 heading north-east towards Salem and the ocean. It was fun to be driven, to enjoy the passing houses and shops without worrying about the traffic. Dake was a good driver, competent and fast.

Traffic was light and they made good time, reaching the outskirts of Salem shortly after noon. Dake took one road, turned on another and soon pulled up against the sand dunes separating the road from the sea.

'All out,' he said. 'We'll have lunch after a hike; we need to warm up.'

Lani nodded, stepping down so that Annalise and Judith-Ann could race ahead.

'I beat!' Judith-Ann sang out, scrambling to the top of the dune.

The girls disappeared over the edge as Lani and Dake began the climb.

'Refreshing!' she gasped when she crested the top and the wind from the sea caught her full in the face.

'You are, too,' Dake said. 'No senseless chatter for mile after mile. I like that.'

Lani smiled, warmed by his praise. She started down.

It was exhilarating to walk the deserted beach in the cold wind. The day was sunny and bright, the water blue and white, the wind steady and cool as it blew from the sea. The girls ran ahead, chasing seagulls, chasing the waves, always careful to keep their feet dry. Lani and Dake walked slowly along, companionably.

'I don't think I've ever been to the beach when it wasn't hot and crowded,' Lani said.

'I love it in all its moods. It refreshes me, after the stress of work. I like it best on days like this— the restless sea, wind, no crowds. I just discovered it, you know. Though we do have a beach on the lake in Chicago.'

'I don't picture you in the open like this. You seem so at home at work, in the office.'

'I like that, too. But this revitalises me, recharges me, has me excited to get back to work, raring to go. What about you? How do you get recharged?'

'Usually by reading a good book, or doing something with Annalise. The girls are getting ahead of us,' she said nervously, picking up the pace to catch up. Dake stopped her, his hand on her arm.

'Lani.'

She looked up. His face was serious.

'I'm not out to get you, nor to hurt you in any way. I'm attracted to you, and think, if you'd just let yourself, you'd be attracted to me. Let's just take it easy, one day at a time.'

Her heart began speeding up.

He was right: if she'd let herself, she would be attracted to him, and she didn't want to be, not a second time.

She took a deep breath, scared of his reaction when she told him. She looked away.

Later, she would tell him later, after lunch. Surely she could have a few hours' enjoyment. And Annalise was having such a good time. She'd tell him later.

Trudging in the sand was hard work, but it kept them warm. In an abrupt change of mood, Lani decided to enjoy what she could of the day, talking with Dake, comparing likes and dislikes. It was a bitter-sweet time. Once she'd thought to have this for always; now she had one day out of time.

They walked for a mile before returning to the jeep. Lani helped gather the picnic things and she and Dake set up in the lee of a dune. Calling the girls, they were all soon eating with enhanced appetites, their walk having sharpened their hunger.

Lani was laughing at something Annalise had said when she looked at Dake to see if he was sharing the moment. His eyes were on her, even as he laughed at the joke.

'Having fun?' he asked.

'Yes, I am. I'm having a good time,' she replied in surprise. Shyly her smile changed. Confused by the look in his eyes, she looked away.

She *was* having fun, carefree, silly fun. It had been a long time. She glanced at her daughter. Had her father stayed with them, would they have often had such fun, had family picnics, done things together? She felt an ache in her heart; she had loved him so much.

But this was today, a different time, a different woman, a different man. She glanced back and smiled. 'I don't think I've eaten this much in years. It's the fresh air and sunshine, I guess.'

'I'm glad you came,' he said softly, reaching up and pulling loose the ribbon from her hair. The waves flowed loose around her face, swirled around her shoulders, lightly moved in the breeze that reached them.

'Why did you do that?' Judith-Ann asked.

'Because I think she looks pretty with her hair like this,' he answered, his eyes never leaving Lani.

'I think she looks pretty all the time,' Annalise said firmly, eyeing him suspiciously.

'I do, too,' was all he said.

'If you girls are finished, help pack up. Then you can go play on the beach some more.'

'I brought a frisbee, if anyone wants to play,' Dake offered.

'Oh, yeah, that will be fun. Come on, Judith-Ann, let's go.'

Quickly putting their rubbish away, and their cups, the two girls ran to the jeep to find the frisbee. Scrambling up the sand dune, they disappeared over the top.

Lani shook her head. 'Where do they find the energy?'

'I don't know, but the man who bottles it to sell will make millions. I think energy is wasted on the young.'

'So you're over the hill, with no energy,' she teased.

'Not as much as when I was younger. But my energy is focused, channelled differently now. Mostly for work.'

'How did you get into the take-over-busting business?' she asked, stretching her legs out before her, leaning back on her hands. It was the closest she could come to asking him what he'd done for the last ten years.

'A strong identity for the underdog, I guess.' He was silent for a moment. 'I liked strategic planning best, and tried to apply it where I felt it would do the most good.'

'So tell me about the jobs you've had.'

'Is this more of the interview process?' He cocked an eyebrow at her.

Lani shrugged, staring at the distant horizon. 'If you like.' Better he think that than that she wanted to know for a more personal reason.

Four Irresistible
Temptations
FREE!

PLUS A MYSTERY GIFT

Temptations offer you all the age-old passion and tenderness of romance, now experienced through very contemporary relationships.

And to introduce to you this powerful and highly charged series, we'll send you **four Temptation romances** absolutely **FREE** when you complete and return this card.

We're so confident that you'll enjoy Temptations that we'll also reserve a subscription to our Reader Service, for you; which means that you'll enjoy...

- **FOUR BRAND NEW NOVELS -** sent direct to you each month (before they're available in the shops).

- **FREE POSTAGE AND PACKING -** we pay all the extras.

- **FREE MONTHLY NEWSLETTER -** packed with special offers, competitions, authors news and much more...

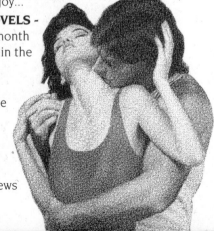

CLAIM THESE GIFTS OVERLEAF

Free Books Certificate

A Free Gift

Return this card now and we'll send you this cuddly Teddy Bear absolutely FREE together with....

A Mystery Gift

We all love mysteries, so as well as the FREE Teddy Bear there's an intriguing FREE gift specially for you.

YES! Please send me **four FREE Temptations** together with my **FREE gifts.** Please also reserve a special Reader Service subscription for me. If I decide to subscribe, I will receive four Temptation romances each month for just £7.00 postage and packing free. If I decide not to subscribe I shall write to you within 10 days. The free books and gifts are mine to keep in any case. **I understood that I am under no obligation whatsoever.** I may cancel or suspend my subscription at any time simply by writing to you. I am over 18 years of age.

MS/MRS/MISS/MR _____ 7A2T

ADDRESS _____

POSTCODE _____ SIGNATURE _____

NO STAMP NEEDED

MILLS & BOON
FREEPOST
P.O. BOX 236
CROYDON
CR9 9EL

Dake complied, launching into anecdotes of his earlier business escapades, entertaining, informative, enlightening. Lani was drawn into his stories, despite her efforts to remain aloof. His rendition mocked his younger self and the mistakes he had made, made light of his accomplishments.

Lani knew, though. She, too, had worked hard, and yet he was a senior vice-president and she was not. Yet.

'So you're a success!' she said.

'Some would say so. I'm more concerned with finding something to do well and have the ability to do it. To some people, success is acquiring things, just to have them—not to enjoy, not to use, just to have.'

'I think as long as you have the basics, and someone to love, to love you, you can be happy without a lot of material things,' Lani said slowly, thinking of the years she'd had with Annalise.

He was silent, the dunes sheltering them from the wind. The roar of the ocean was only a soft murmur on the far side. It was warm and pleasant in the shelter.

'It doesn't come to everyone, though,' he said. 'I lived with someone once,' he added unexpectedly.

She tensed, swivelled to look at him.

He grinned self-deprecatingly. 'It was years and years ago, when I was a kid. It didn't work out. It's odd—I don't remember her, wouldn't know her if I passed her in the street. I have flashes of

memory, that's all. Maybe she was one who
wanted more than I could provide.'

Lani was very still, almost afraid to breathe.
He really didn't remember her! She'd never forgotten one minute of their time together and he
didn't even remember her!

CHAPTER EIGHT

LANI'S throat went dry as the coldness seeped into her heart. The roar in her ears was not that of the nearby ocean, but of her own heart, pumping double time in the shock of what Dake said.

She was cold, cold and numb with the realisation of it all. As she had grown to suspect, the marriage was a farce, a sham. He had never been married, just lived with a girl. One, moreover, whom he would not recognise if he met again. One he *had* not recognised when he had met her again.

And she had remembered every bit of their time together, had cherished it, even while despising the way he had left her. She felt sick, nausea rising in her throat. She wanted to go home, away from this man, to be by herself.

There would be no confrontation today. She just wanted to get away.

'Are you all right?' His voice penetrated the roar in her ears.

Avoiding his eyes, she nodded, standing up, dusting the sand from her jeans.

Then she shook her head. 'No, actually, I don't feel very well. Would you mind very much if we went now? I'll... I'll lie down and be fine once I get home.'

With his assistance, Lani quickly repacked the picnic basket, and, still avoiding looking directly at him, climbed the dune to call the girls. Before long they were heading back to Boston.

Lani huddled in the corner of the front seat, staring blindly ahead. Her mind in turmoil, she resolved not to think about anything, until she reached the safety of her own home. But unbidden the thoughts tumbled in. She had been right at the first: he was trouble and she should stay away. She had been fooling herself. But she had wanted to be with him, see how he had matured, what he had become. She didn't want to be drawn to him, attracted by him again, not after what he had done, but she was.

He had been her husband, or so she'd always thought, and she still felt the pull he had always had for her. Did she want to fall in love with him again? She rather thought she had never fallen out of love with him, despite his desertion. If he courted her now, would she be able to trust him? Give her life into his keeping a second time, knowing how the first time had ended?

Yet why did she even think he would consider courting her? They had lived together, for God's sake, and he didn't even remember her name!

He reached over and clasped her hand, his touch like fire. Lani snatched hers away. When Dake looked puzzled, she reached up to refasten her hair into a pony-tail. He did not pursue the issue, but was thoughtful throughout the rest of the ride.

When they reached her apartment, she flung open the passenger door. 'We'll be fine from here. Thanks for the picnic,' she said, motioning for Annalise and Judith-Ann to get out. They thanked him nicely for the picnic, but his eyes were on Lani.

'I'll see you tomorrow,' he said, ominously, to Lani's ears.

'Yes...no...I don't know.' She avoided his eyes.

She slammed the car door and turned up the walkway, tears threatening. It had started out such a good day, and had ended disastrously. She blinked her eyes, and opened the door.

'You girls can play for a little longer, then Judith-Ann will have to get home,' she said, running up the stairs, longing for the sanctuary of her bedroom. Once behind the door, she relaxed, the tears spilling down her cheeks. She pushed off and flung herself on her bed, the ache in her heart familiar, a long-time companion.

Her bedroom door slammed open, hitting the wall behind it with force.

'What the devil's the matter with you, Lani?' Dake's angry voice followed.

She sat up slowly, brushing the tears from her face, turning reluctantly to face him. His features softened slightly when he saw her tear-stained cheeks, but he didn't say anything.

'I don't feel good,' she said, her nerves taut.

'I don't think so. I think this is more of the runaway syndrome you do so well. Are you upset because I told you I lived with someone once?'

She looked down at the floor; he was too perceptive.

Sighing, Dake came into the room, sat beside her on the bed and reached out to take her hands in his. She looked up at him, his eyes staring back at her with the intensity she knew so well.

'I'm attracted to you, and once or twice I think it's been returned. I want to get to know you, see where we can go together. You are a beautiful woman, smart, hard-working, but not given to much relaxation and fun, as far as I can see. And yet any time I try to reach you as a man wants to reach a woman, you turn away. Why, Lani? Why?'

She shrugged, unable to tell him.

'You have to get over the bastard you married, not let his desertion stop you from moving on, from having other friendships, other lovers. Don't sacrifice a chance for happiness for the sake of something that happened ten years ago. People change, times change. Give me a chance.'

She stared at him. Did he really not remember her? Or were his words somehow designed to reassure her while not admitting the guilt, not admitting desertion? Could she give him a chance, see what might develop? Could she ever trust him again?

The tears started again, spilling over. She made no effort to wipe them away. 'I hurt so badly, and for so long, I thought at one point I would die. I loved my husband quite desperately; I couldn't stand that kind of pain again.'

'Trust me on this, Lani. I won't let you down.'

As he had once before.

'Don't rush me,' she whispered, drawing away from him, afraid to let herself go. What if she asked him about the past? She shied away from that. She just wanted him to leave.

'Please, Dake, just go.'

His face tightened, but he nodded acquiescence. 'All right, I'll back off for a while. But not forever, Lani. Not forever.'

Lani avoided Dake whenever she could at work the next week. Monday was easy; they both had things to catch up on because of their absence. Tuesday wasn't as easy, but she gave her secretary instructions to interrupt her if Dake came into her office. She knew she ran a risk of Stacey starting gossip over the instructions, but recklessly didn't care. She didn't want to be alone with Dake just yet.

By Thursday, she knew he was getting frustrated. He cornered her in the hallway just after a meeting with John.

'How about having lunch with me today?' he asked, one arm raised against the wall, the other holding his folder and pen, his body shielding her.

'I'm busy,' she said, avoiding his eyes and trying to side-step around him. But he had her imprisoned.

'Dammit, Lani, what gives?' He reached out to hold her arm. 'Whenever we're together, you're trying to get away. All I want to do is make some friends here in Boston. But you are always tightening up and turning away.'

She looked down at his hand holding her, his skin warm and firm against her arm, those same hands that had once held her in love and passion, that had caressed her, brought her to the heights of ecstasy and beyond.

She glanced to his mouth, remembering how intoxicating his kisses had been, heady, exciting, teasing, fulfilling. How his warm lips had brought her alive, kissing lips, trailing nibbles down her neck to her shoulders, then to the gentle slopes of her breasts. How she'd flared into passion when they captured her rosy tip or trailed fire along her breasts. His lips had always been able to bring her skin to tingling awareness, sensitive delight.

She looked away and tried to withdraw from his touch.

'I'm not always running away. But I do have things to do, sometimes.' Thank God mind-reading was not one of his abilities. 'Besides——' she bravely looked up into his eyes '—we'll see each other Saturday night, remember? I really have to go now, Dake.'

It was not getting better. She had thought being around him would dull her senses, that she'd be able to treat him in a businesslike manner, as one of the other guys. But she couldn't. Her traitorous body leaped in recognition of his, her heart pounded out a signal to him for his response. She couldn't forget their past, ached for it. If she couldn't control her emotions, she'd better seriously think of another job.

*   *   *

It was Friday afternoon and Lani was reviewing communiqués for release on Monday. Only half paying attention to the job at hand, she was also trying to decide what to wear for the next evening's gathering.

'Excuse me, do you know where I can find Dake Morgan?' A throaty voice interrupted Lani's train of thought.

She looked up. Before her stood a tall woman, fashionably dressed, her short dark hair sleek and daring, her make-up heavier than Lani liked, but on her it was striking. She looked like a model from *Vogue*. Lani took an instant dislike to her.

'His office is two down on your right,' she answered cordially.

'So the receptionist told me, but he's not there.' She smiled perfect teeth and stepped into Lani's office, hand outstretched. 'I should introduce myself, I'm Stephanie Wilcox, Dake's fiancée.'

Lani stood, as if in a dream and shook hands, dazed at the news. Dake had never hinted... It struck her again, the pain and disappointment sharp. *She could not trust him*. His actions had never suggested he was already engaged!

'Do have a seat, Miss Wilcox; I'll see if I can have him located.' Lani spoke quickly to Stacey, asking her to find Dake, then turned back to her visitor.

'I'm Lani Williams. Dake is new here; I didn't realise he was engaged.' She sat down rather abruptly, her legs refusing to hold her.

Stephanie laughed throatily and shook her head slightly, a small moue on her lips. 'It's not official, yet. Dake is such a rake, he does like to play the field. I'm sure he's been flirting with all the pretty secretaries here. But we have an understanding, and once we are married he won't have any reason to look elsewhere. I'm here to spend the weekend with him, see the sights of Boston. He's been away too long.'

'He's not been flirting with the secretaries, that I know of,' Lani said to reassure her. *Only flirting with me.* What reaction would that cause? 'Have you been to Boston before?' she asked politely.

'No, if you live in New York, there's no need to travel to Boston. New York has everything I want. But Dake *would* come to Boston.' She frowned then quickly schooled her face so there were no wrinkles. 'This is a poky little place, isn't it?' she sighed. 'Dake could have worked for Daddy. He's a financier on Wall Street. But Dake's headstrong, insisted this is what he wanted to do.'

Lani took offence at the denigration of her beloved Sanderson's. Before she could protest, however, Dake appeared in the door.

'Lani, Stacey said you were looking for me?'

'No, darling, I was.' Stephanie rose and greeted Dake with a long kiss, her arms wrapping themselves around his neck. He pulled them down and stepped back a step, his eyes flickering to Lani, back to Stephanie.

'What are you doing here, Steph?'

'Why, darling, I came to see how you were getting along in Boston all by yourself. Aren't you glad to see me?'

Lani looked down at the papers on her desk. Couldn't they have their reunion in Dake's office, instead of hers? She didn't like the shaft of jealousy that pierced her at the sight of Stephanie in Dake's arms. She had no business getting mixed up with him again. Hadn't his actions ten years ago shown her that? She knew she could not trust him, why play with fire?

'I'm up to my back teeth in work, Steph. This is not a good weekend for a visit.'

'Darling, you need a break from work. Any weekend I come is a good weekend. We can discover Boston together.'

'We can discuss this in my office.' He put his arm around Stephanie's shoulders and ushered her none too gently from the room.

Lani sat staring out into the empty hall for several minutes, trying to put together what she'd just seen and heard.

She knew Dake wasn't a monk; he was too sexy, virile, demonstrative. Why shouldn't he have a girlfriend? Why should Lani think he had remained faithful to her? Her ego was bruised. She didn't like Dake's fiancée. She didn't like the fact that he had a fiancée! And where did that put her? A light flirt to help pass the time until *Steph* arrived? She hated the thought!

CHAPTER NINE

'AH, THE woman of my dreams has arrived, looking ravishing, I might add.'

Lani paused in the large foyer, the glittering chandelier illuminating the gorgeous finery of Boston society. The butler took her coat and turned towards the cloakroom. Lani turned to frown at Joel. It was not he whom she wanted to impress. She had come to the Sorenson ball only because John expected it. She dreaded seeing Dake and Stephanie here.

'I have been awaiting your arrival with bated breath, and a lot of fear that you wouldn't come at all.'

'Joel, didn't you bring a date?'

'What, and miss the one chance I might have to take you home? I figure tonight I can bide my time, while you are imbibing the bubbly. When the moment is right, I strike. And offer the fair, tipsy damsel a safe ride home.'

She laughed at his absurdity. 'Honestly, Joel, I don't plan to get tipsy. And I have transportation home.'

'You drove?'

'No, but I already arranged for a cab. Is everyone from the office here?'

'I've seen John and Nora, Mark and Beth and Judy and Bob. No one else yet. I like your dress.

Can I at least look my fill?' He leered at her boyishly, his eyes travelling the length of her.

Lani had worn a long formal dress of navy taffeta; fragile lace covered her shoulders and arms, and the underdress fitted her figure like a glove, flaring to swirl about her ankles. Her hair was done up with curls cascading down her neck, giving her a softer, younger look. She had dressed with care for this event, the first one of interest to her in over ten years. She wanted to look her best, but refused to admit to herself the reason why.

'Joel, you're just doing this for the thrill of the chase. If I went out with you, we'd be bored to tears in about an hour. Go and find a pretty young girl who will think you're great.'

'And you don't? I'm crushed.' He leaned over and kissed her cheek. 'You're probably right, but it's such fun, and just think, one day you might say yes. Come on and we'll find some of the bubbly, check out the buffet table and let everyone from the office see how much more fun work could be if we dressed up each day.'

She laughed at the idea, moving along with him, her eyes darting here and there, looking for Dake. Dake and Stephanie, she corrected herself, though, if Joel was correct, they were not here yet.

'Did you see Dake's girl?' Joel asked as they reached the buffet table. Lani took a moment longer than necessary looking over the people circulating.

'Yes, I met her yesterday, at the office.'

'Me too. What a looker! If I had someone like
that I would not have moved to Boston alone.
Are they coming tonight?'

'I don't know. I assumed so, since we were all
rather strongly urged to attend.' She hadn't considered that they wouldn't come. John probably
wouldn't mind; Dake was new to the firm, and
with an unexpected out-of-town guest he could
be excused for not attending. The evening suddenly seemed dull.

They helped themselves to a few hors-d'oeuvres
and moved through the crowd to find their co-
workers. Conversation was casual as they com-
mented on the number of people who had turned
out, the fine buffet and the band they could hear
warming up in the large ballroom beyond.

The cream of Boston society was present, for
the Sorenson Charity Ball was an annual affair
that guaranteed to be the event of the autumn
season. Everyone wanted to attend. The funds
raised went to several charities in Boston, with
matching donations from the Sorenson family
itself.

Lani lapsed into silence when Nora Harrington
began telling them about her new redecoration
scheme. Glancing around at the exquisitely
gowned and coiffed women, the handsome men
in evening dress, Lani marvelled at her own at-
tendance. It was different, even exciting, for one
night. But she didn't think she'd like it all the
time.

She would mingle with some of the people she recognised, be on her best social behaviour as a reflection of Sanderson's. Then she could leave.

Excusing herself at a suitable change of topic, Lani went to talk to one of the men from Sorenson's she had dealt with at the Security and Exchange Commission hearing. She met his wife, heard the latest on their company, and moved on.

She suddenly saw Dake across the room. He was standing alone, holding a glass of champagne, looking around. She knew exactly when he saw her. He walked through the crowd as if it didn't exist. She felt a mingling of apprehension and anticipation surge through her body as she watched him draw closer. He looked handsome in his black dinner-jacket, the white shirt dazzling, his tan not yet faded.

As he drew near he smiled, that heart-stopping smile he had, with his eyes softening, his teeth white against his skin.

'Hello,' he said, stopping before her. Too close.

'Hello.' She was suddenly breathless, nervous, wanting to move away, wanting to move closer.

'You came alone?' he asked.

'Yes, as I said I would. You brought Stephanie?'

He waved his hand vaguely. 'She's somewhere around. How's Annalise?'

'She's fine. You should be introducing Stephanie around.'

'Dammit, is Stephanie all you want to talk about?'

'I thought she'd be what you would want to talk about.'

'Well, I don't. It wasn't my idea for her to come chasing up to Boston.' His eyes narrowed as he gazed down at her, taking in her dress, her hair.

'Doesn't Stephanie share your liking of Boston?' she asked carefully, eyes ahead.

Dake tilted her chin up to face him.

'Let's hear it. What did Steph say?'

Lani licked her lips, suddenly wishing she had not said anything, not wanting it confirmed. 'I don't know what you mean.'

His fingers were warm. Her face tilted as if to receive a kiss. Lani should step away, but she couldn't.

He sighed, 'It's obvious she made mention of something; you certainly have us paired up.'

'She did mention that she was your fiancée.'

He stared at Lani for a long moment, his face unreadable. Finally he replied.

'Stephanie would like to be. Her father would like that, too. But when and if the time comes for me to take a wife, *I'll* choose. And I'll make sure the woman knows and the whole world. I have never asked Stephanie to marry me.'

But will you? she asked silently. There had to be something between them for Stephanie to think they were engaged.

'Lani.'

She started, spilling a little of her champagne.

'You seem nervous, Lani.'

'You are disturbing to my peace of mind.'

'I'd rather be disturbing to your heart,' he said, gently resting one warm finger over her heart.

She felt the touch as a burning shaft, piercing her dress, piercing her skin, its heat penetrating directly to her heart.

She began trembling as he slowly trailed his finger across the gentle swell of her breast, down towards the dark shadow of her cleavage.

'Stop that!' She snatched his finger, pulling his hand away from her. They were in the middle of a crowded reception-room, for heaven's sake! She chanced a glance around. No one seemed to be paying any attention to them.

He captured her hand, raising each finger to his mouth, lips caressing each tip in turn. Between each small kiss he murmured for her ears alone, 'You are irresistible, and delectable. You look ravishing in that dress, though I'd like to get you away from here, ease it from your shoulders and see what loveliness you have hidden. Take you to my place, light a fire and slowly disrobe before its warmth.'

Lani stared at him, mesmerised by his seductive voice, the tantalising picture he painted in her mind.

'I'd like to see your silky skin in the flickering firelight, its softness reflecting the glow of the fire, the paleness capturing the rosy radiance from the flames.' His thumb traced gentle circles on the sensitive pulse of her wrist. Lani felt as if she were slowly dissolving, as she was drawn into the tempting fantasy.

'Then I'd take you in my arms and make slow, exquisite love to you all night long.' He placed a warm kiss in the palm of her hand, one on the sensitive spot in her wrist.

Lani caught her breath, held it. The picture was so reminiscent of the many loving nights they had shared when she'd thought they were married. She wondered if he was teasing her; was this his way to bring up the past? It had to stop. It was madness; it would lead nowhere.

She looked up at him, feeling drugged with the persuasiveness of his words, the images he conjured in her mind.

'Now you are beginning to sound like Joel.'

'I'm nothing like Joel,' he growled softly in her ear.

'He's always talking about making passionate love to me,' she said, trying to step back. Joel never made her feel weak this way. Never had his words alone almost caused her to sink in a pool of molten delight.

'I'm more man than Joel will ever be. Come with me, and I'll show you the difference,' Dake murmured, holding her eyes with his.

Lani flushed in panic. He was moving too fast for her, was too sure of himself. She didn't know where she was. Should she tell him? Tell him she didn't know what game he was playing but that she and he had once played marriage? See what he said. Was he only toying with her? Leading her on, only to disappoint her once again when he grew tired of the game?

She needed to know. She wanted to know what Stephanie was to him. What was he doing talking to her, as he was with his *fiancée* at the same party?

'Oh, here you are, Dake, I wanted you to meet Nora.' John Harrington interrupted Lani's confused thoughts.

Dake's smile was mocking as he turned from Lani to greet the president and his wife. The present snapped into focus. The reception was crowded, people milled about them. Jewellery glittered in the light, beautiful gowns rustled softly as women moved, the air was lightly scented with the mingling of all the perfumes.

Lani gave a sigh of relief and stepped back another step. For the moment Lani thought only of escape. She fled for the buffet table, wanting a moment to collect herself, to lose herself in the anonymity of the crowd.

As the evening progressed, Lani kept a wary eye out for Dake, watched as he was introduced to group after group, always keeping several people between herself and him. She was not going to be caught by him again.

Stephanie was holding court near one of the doors to the ballroom, splendid in a crimson red strapless gown. Lani stopped to watch her flirt with the men who flocked around, curious as to Dake's reaction. When she tried to judge it, she was stymied. Dake seemed totally unaware of Stephanie, yet he always seemed to know exactly where Lani was. Every time she looked over at him, he was watching her. Had Stephanie made

it all up? Doubt and confusion worried Lani's
mind.

Lani was talking with old Edgar Higgams of
Forsythe and Smythe when Dake appeared at her
side.

'Excuse me, sir. Lani has me down for this
dance.'

Before she could protest, he gracefully cut her
away from Mr Higgams and drew her to the
ballroom.

'I don't want to dance,' she said, trying to pull
her arm from his firm grasp without making a
scene. His hold was too strong, his hand warm
against her arm, the lace no impediment to his
searing touch.

'But you haven't danced all evening, and the
band is really quite good.'

'Dake, let me go, I don't want to dance,' she
hissed, anxious to escape, not trusting herself to
dance with him.

'Relax, Lani, it's only a dance.' He turned to
face her, drawing her into his arms, moving
smoothly to the strains of the waltz.

As they swayed to slow, dreamy music, Lani
tried to hold herself away from him, but his arms
drew her closer, until she was fitted against his
body. She stumbled, unable to concentrate. Her
traitorous body recognised Dake's and reacted
accordingly.

'Nice party, don't you think?' she said to cover
the pounding of her heart which he must certainly hear.

'I don't want bright party chatter now. I just
want to hold you, move with you. Maybe later,
who knows? My place?'

As he drew her closer, Lani was instantly intently aware of every move he made. His legs
brushed against hers, his chest was a solid wall
against which her soft breasts were crushed. His
hand against her back was hot, pulsating with
sensuous movement, causing little waves of en-
ticement to march up her spine. The scent of his
aftershave was musky, the same kind he wore all
those years ago. The scent transformed her to the
shy first-year college student she once had been,
caught up in the delights of first love.

The muscles of his shoulders moved beneath
her hand, filling her with the desire to explore
them more fully, to move her fingertips against
his firm warm flesh, trail them into the thick dark
hair, feel the texture of his skin against her own.
She knew if she tried to break free he could hold
her with little effort, so why try?

She threw caution to the wind and decided to
enjoy herself with no guilt and no qualms. It was,
as he had said, only a dance.

The music grew softer and slower, the lights
dimmed and Dake drew her closer still, resting
his forehead on hers, his lips millimetres from
her own, his breath mingling with hers. Lani
wondered if she could lose herself in the deep,
dark depths of his eyes? It was as if they were
the only two people in the room, lost in a world
of their own, floating on clouds, swaying in time
to the soft, slow music.

'I want to know you better, Lani. And I don't mean the professional woman at work. I want to know the personal, private womanly things you like to do, to know how you feel about things. Learn what you like, what you dislike.'

His hand caressed her fingers, his other hand moved in slow seductive circles along her spine, moved lower, forcing her against him, the bandages still on two fingers not interfering. Lani shivered, giving in to the growing desire budding deep within her.

'Don't,' she whispered, as they swayed to the music. Dake was skilful at keeping them away from the other couples. They could have been alone in the ballroom.

'I want to feel your silky skin against mine, learn all the secret places that you have, so they're not secret to me. Learn what brings you pleasure, what you dislike. I want to make love with you far into the night and waken with you in the morning to start the day together.' His voice was soft in her ear, hypnotising.

'Don't,' she whispered, 'we can't.' Her eyes darted around, frantically seeking escape from the tantalising images he invoked.

'Why not?' He placed a feathery soft kiss at the edge of her mouth. 'I'd like to see your shining hair undone from these curls, pretty as they are, spread over your shoulders, spread all over my pillow. I want to run my fingers through the fine strands and feel it fall gently against your neck.'

'Dake, please!' Her voice was agonised. Heat suffused her whole body as the longing grew.

The slow bud of desire opened to a full-fledged burning that demanded satisfaction. Lani had to stop the madness before it consumed her.

'We can't,' she repeated. Why wasn't her voice firm, decisive?

'Sure, we can. Just let yourself go. I want you, Lani, I've wanted you from the first moment I saw you. I've wanted you every moment we've been together. I feel there's something between us; you must feel it, too. It's too strong to be denied.'

Lani closed her eyes. Without his support, she would have fallen to the floor. She did feel it, but she dared not admit it.

'What about Stephanie?' she asked. He drew back and frowned down at her.

'What about Stephanie? I thought we'd settled that. I'll have Joel take her back to her hotel. He'd love to do it and it would take a burden off me.'

'I don't think Stephanie considers herself a burden.'

'Stephanie considers herself entirely too much,' he said roughly. 'It was her idea to come here, not mine. I'll tell you all about Stephanie on the ride home. Are you ready to go?'

'No,' she said. 'We can't leave. Anyway, I'm not going with you.' Her voice wasn't as strong as she wished.

Dake said nothing, ignoring her protestations. He moved them in time to the music, drawing

her close to him, a constant source of delight as
he moved around the floor, his hands caressing
her as they swayed. She felt relaxed, desirable and
desired. Gradually Dake manoeuvred them
towards the slightly opened french door, and
danced her out on to the patio.

'Dake! It's freezing out here.' Lani was abruptly snatched from her reverie by the cold.

'I have a way to warm you up,' he growled,
pulling her back into the shadows, his mouth
eagerly seeking hers.

With the first explosive touch, Lani was lost.
It was the old delight she remembered from years
ago. Forgetting all else, Lani gave in to the memories and returned Dake's kiss measure for
measure. It was as if she had come home again.

Dake's kiss brought her alive, as passion
dormant for years now flared to meet his. Her
fingers found the thickness of his hair, revelling
in the feel of it. She had longed to thread her
fingers through it for ages. She gripped the
strength of his shoulders, feeling heat from his
body, the muscles beneath the clothing. Endless
delight and pleasure coursed through her body
as his kiss deepened. His hands roamed over her
back, keeping her close, probing the sensitive
areas along her spine that brought her trembling
desire.

She didn't want the moment to end, she wanted
to float along on sensual delights he evoked, to
float on to heaven and the dawn.

'Dake?' a throaty voice called. 'Dake, are you
out here?'

'Dammit.' He drew back and thrust Lani into the darkness beside the door.

'I'm here, Stephanie,' he answered, straightening and stepping away from Lani.

Lani's eyes widened in consternation. Confrontation with the wronged fiancée was not something she wanted. Quickly looking around, she found no means of escape.

'Darling, whatever are you doing out here? Are you alone?' Stephanie's voice sharpened. 'Who is that?'

'It's Lani Williams, Miss Wilcox. I...I was feeling faint, and Dake brought me outside for fresh air.' Lani marvelled that her voice was so calm, so normal.

'It's freezing out here,' Stephanie said sharply.

Lani's eyes darted to Dake. She had voiced similar concerns. She smiled; he was right, he had warmed her up.

'I must be coming down with something; I don't feel cold at all,' she replied, looking away from the gleam in his eye.

'Maybe you should go home,' Stephanie suggested, looking suspiciously from one to the other.

'I think you're right; I will go home.'

'I'll take you,' Dake said quickly.

'I can get a cab.' Lani might as well have saved her breath.

'Stephanie, I'll get one of the men from work to take you back to your hotel.'

'I don't need you to take me home; I can manage.' Lani just wanted to get away.

'We'll all go. I'm tired anyway, and you might
want a woman along, in case you start feeling
unwell again.' Stephanie smiled. 'Dake, darling,
why don't you get a cab for us all? I'll wait with
Ms Williams.'

Lani took the initiative. 'An excellent idea. I'll
get my wrap.' She pushed away from the wall and,
head held high, marched into the ballroom and
through to the cloakroom.

Dake went to call a cab and Stephanie stopped
for a moment to chat with someone she'd met.

When Lani joined Dake in the foyer, they were
alone. He smiled at her, his eyes dark and
fathomless. Gently he reached out to lightly trace
her lips with his thumb.

'A little swollen. I want to kiss you again,' he
said frankly. His look was of pure desire.

Lani swayed towards him. She, too, wanted his
kiss.

'Sorry to keep you. Is the cab here?' Stephanie
was wrapped in mink, oblivious to the electrified
air in the foyer.

'Just arriving.' Dake's face was impassive, his
manner courteous.

The next half-hour was forever dim in Lani's
memory. She refused to look at either Dake or
Stephanie, bore with them only until the cab
stopped at her doorway.

'I'll be fine; sorry I can't invite you in, but I
want to go straight to bed.' She bit her tongue,
the image of Dake in bed with her flashed before
her eyes. 'Thank you for the ride.'

She almost ran up the short pathway, her key out so as not to delay her escape. Once the door was closed behind her, she leaned against it, slowly sinking to a heap on the floor.

What a fool she'd made of herself. She knew she couldn't trust him, couldn't rely on him. How could she give in to kisses and sweet talk when she knew he played around, knew his fiancée was at the same party? When she closed her eyes, though, she didn't feel like a fool; she felt as if she was nineteen again, and in love.

CHAPTER TEN

SUNDAY was a balmy autumn day. Annalise played outside with some friends while Lani caught up on tasks around the house. She wanted time to ponder the situation between her and Dake.

She remembered the frantic days when he had not returned, calling hospitals, the Boston police. And finally the call to the private detective. Trying desperately to find her husband. Terrified he'd been injured or killed. Never knowing what happened. Still not knowing.

Work at Sanderson's was proving more and more difficult. Lani, knowing who Dake was and constantly alert for the time he'd acknowledge who she was, bring up the past, bring out all the hurt and fears she tried so hard to suppress. Lani found it increasingly difficult to be with him and not talk of the past. Trying to avoid him, however, was impossible. There were meetings and conferences to attend, information needed for work on the Forscue project or the pending trip to Washington.

Then there was the time away from work. The beach outing, the night they'd made brownies. Dancing at Sorenson's last night. Her senses tingled in remembered delight of their dancing. She blushed, finding herself daydreaming. She

was supposed to be deciding what to do about
the situation, not remembering past delights.

Dake had ignored her evasive techniques, or
been amused by them. She was reluctant to be
very overt in her evasion; she did not want to
give rise to speculation and gossip from the others
about her reactions to this very disturbing man.

He did not appear at all perturbed to be with
her; instead seemed to delight in pursuing her,
catching her unawares. Was Stephanie right: was
he a womaniser? He didn't seem to take any hint
that she would prefer him elsewhere.

By the end of the morning, Lani was no further
along in her thought process than when she'd
started. She'd just take one day at a time.

She was restless, edgy. Maybe she needed
something to take her mind off the problem.
She'd go into work and catch up on a few things.
There was always so much to do.

Leaving Annalise at Judith-Ann's, Lani drove
to work. The office was quiet, cool, the normal
hum of business absent on Sunday. Lani glanced
around as she walked quickly to her office. It
was a little spooky.

She was soon engrossed in work and forgot her
nervousness. Then she heard a sound, a door
closing somewhere. Her heart began tripping; was
someone else here? She held her breath, straining
to listen, trying to determine what it was she
heard.

When she heard a low tuneless whistling, she
relaxed. It couldn't be a thief, or worse. Must be
another staff member. She picked up the bro-

chure she was working on and began editing.
Some time later she heard the whistle again. The
sound stopped and she looked up.

Dake Morgan paused, filling her doorway.

'What are you doing here?' Lani blurted out,
surprised to see him. If she had thought about
it, she would have expected him to be with
Stephanie. In fact, she had thought that.

'Could ask you the same thing except it's obvious. You're catching up on some things. I was
working at home and needed a file I'd forgotten.'

She saw the manila folder in his hand.

He leaned against the jamb and watched her,
content with saying nothing.

Lani grew flushed under his regard. She
fidgeted with papers on her desk, trying to ignore
him. To no avail.

'What are you working on?' he asked, pushing
himself off the wall to come to her desk.

'Reviewing a brochure to include in the next
mailing to Forscue's stockholders.'

Dake perched on her desk, craning his neck to
see what she held.

'I was reviewing the game plan for this
project—found a couple of places where our
attack is weak. Want to review it with me, bounce
some ideas off each other?'

Lani looked up. She loved strategic planning,
coming up with ideas, no matter how far-fetched,
to see what they could build from, what the final
results were.

'Sure, sounds good.'

'Let's go, then.'

'Go? Where?'

'My place. I told you I was doing stuff there and forgot this folder.'

'I thought you meant here,' Lani faltered.

The familiar glint in his eyes told her he was amused with her. 'Scared, Ms Williams?'

She was, but she would never admit it to him. Tilting her chin determinedly, she rose.

'I'm ready.' She stacked the brochure papers on the corner of her desk and grabbed her bag. 'I'll follow you.'

She was not going to lose that bit of independence.

As she followed Dake towards Copley Square, she felt excitement build. Soon she would see where Dake lived, where he spent his time when away from her. Away from work, she amended.

She was not surprised to find he lived in one of the glass and steel towers that overlooked downtown Boston. She parked where he indicated and went to the security door. In only a moment he came up from the underground garage to admit her.

The apartment was large. The big window on the living-room wall overlooked downtown. It would be pretty after dark with all the lights. She glanced around the tastefully decorated room. It looked like a showplace. But not a home.

Dake took her bag and jacket, tossing them with his on a chair by the door.

'Down here.' He walked down the short hall to a study.

To Lani, it looked like an office. He had a phone on the desk, shelves of books on finance, budgeting, marketing and business law. The desk was covered with folders and papers. There was a large writing board on one wall, and notations and flowcharts filled two-thirds of it. Two chairs and a small love-seat completed the furnishings.

The view from the window was the same as from the living-room, though the window was smaller.

Lani sat gingerly on the edge of her chair, wondering if this had been such a good idea after all.

'Where's Annalise?' Dake asked, tossing the manila folder on the desk.

'At Judith-Ann's.'

'She's a cute kid; does she do well in school?'

'Yes, she's a good student, yet not a bookworm. She's quite active.'

Dake sat sprawled out on the love-seat, his legs stretched out before him, head resting on the back. He watched Lani from half-closed eyes.

Sexy eyes, she thought involuntarily.

'Stop looking at me,' she said quietly.

'I like looking at you. You're a pretty woman, with a pretty little girl. How old is she?'

'Nine, almost ten.'

He asked a few more questions about Annalise, giving Lani courage to enquire about his own personal life.

'I was surprised you were working. I thought you'd be spending time with Stephanie.' She avoided meeting his eyes.

'She's gone.'

'Gone?'

'I put her on a flight back to New York about an hour ago. She won't be back.'

So you dumped her too, flashed in Lani's mind. She had not liked Stephanie, but she could be sorry for her.

Her nerves jangled; she jumped up and stood before the writing board, pretending to study what he'd written.

'Are you always this nervous around men?' he asked, moving silently to stand beside her.

'No, just you.' She side-stepped.

He reached out and turned her around to face him, a devilish glint in his eye.

'That's most provocative.'

'It's not meant to be.' A moment of panic flashed through Lani.

'Now, how can I make you less nervous?' he mused, his thumbs rubbing her upper arms gently.

She wrinkled her nose at him, 'Treat me the way you treat Joel. I thought we were here to work.'

He paused, an arrested look on his face, staring at her with intense concentration. He seemed in a trance.

She looked up. 'What?'

He shook his head and dropped his hands, moving away.

'Nothing—I thought I remembered someone. It's gone. You're right, we're here to work.'

Lani found the next few hours exhilarating. Dake had a quick mind, his ideas and strategies were dynamic and forceful. He had intuitions she'd not considered and made a solid argument for them. Together they rehashed the plans, formulated different tactics and contingency positions. The time flew by.

Lani was conscious of Dake on a physical level, even as her mind challenged his. She watched as he thrust his fingers through his hair when making a point. She longed to run her fingers through his thick dark hair. His body moved smoothly as he paced the room, his movements almost graceful as he gestured while he talked.

She caught a glimpse of the time, startled at how late it was.

'I've got to go.' She stood up suddenly. She hadn't expected to be gone this long. Annalise would be wondering where she was.

Dake stood too, moved over near her.

'Have dinner with me,' he said.

'No. I can't.'

He reached out and gently brushed back a strand of hair that had worked itself loose from her pony-tail.

'We'll take Annalise, too. What had you planned for dinner?'

She stared at him, eyes wide. Why did he always make her feel so naïve and young?

He sighed. 'Lani, why do you instantly say no to everything I propose?'

'I don't,' she said, knowing he was right.

'Pizza—you both like that. Come on, we'll get Annalise.'

He laced his fingers through hers and drew her down the hall.

Lani resisted only a second, then followed, emotions mixed up. She wanted to be with him. She didn't want to further their time together. She didn't know what she wanted.

Dinner was fun. The strain Lani had anticipated did not materialise. Dake was easygoing, impersonal. He talked to Annalise, joked with Lani and smoothly set the pace he wanted. Lani sat back and enjoyed herself.

When Dake gave Annalise a handful of coins to play the videos, she was thrilled.

'Don't leave until I'm done,' Annalise instructed as she danced away from the table.

Dake grinned at Lani. 'She's quite a kid. You must be so proud of her.'

Lani smiled and nodded. 'I am.'

He reached out and took one of her hands, holding it in one of his, tracing her fingers, the soft skin at her wrist with his other hand, his eyes fixed on their joined hands.

Lani found it difficult to breathe. His touch was tantalising, erotic. She wanted to fling herself into his arms and have him kiss her the way he had last night.

'What are you thinking about?' Dake's eyes gleamed in the light, he had a smile on his lips.

Lani blushed. She could not tell him she'd been mooning around like a love-struck schoolgirl.

'This and that.'

'Like what?'

'Like we've got to be going. Tomorrow is a school day and Annalise still needs a bath. Thank you for dinner.'

'Running away?' he taunted.

I leave that to you, she thought bitterly.

'Just going home.'

Lani was surprised to find Dake following her as she drove home. He pulled in the drive behind her, climbed out of his jeep and met her in the garage.

'Wanted to make sure you got home safely,' he said.

'We're just fine, thanks.'

'Lani, send Annalise in for her bath,' Dake's voice urged.

She didn't argue, nor ask why. Her heart began pounding, the blood sang through her veins.

When Annalise had left, Dake pulled Lani into the shadows of the garage, away from the glare of the streetlight. He drew her into his arms, his lips finding hers.

She melted against him and gave herself up to the pleasure of his touch. This was what she wanted, she had longed for this since last night. She had longed for it for ten years! Lani tried to track the emotions and feelings that churned in her head, but lost the ability as the ecstasy he evoked filled her being.

His lips were warm, persuasive, hard and sexy. His kiss deepened, inflaming her. As he tightened his hold, she strained to get closer. His touch was a delight, her passion flared, she wanted more.

He kissed her cheek, her eyes, tilted her head back to expose her soft throat.

'I've been wanting this all afternoon. It was too hard to concentrate on business with you so close, and so out of reach,' he murmured as he tasted her, his mouth moving against the sensitive spots beneath her ear, back to her lips. 'Wanted to make love to you all afternoon. Forget Sanderson's and Forscue and Sorenson's...wanted you.'

Lani pushed back; this was madness. She could not let herself get intoxicated on a few kisses. Wonderful though they were.

'No, Dake. I...I need to go in.' She avoided his eyes. He dropped his arms slowly, a puzzled, half-angry look on his face.

'Lani...'

'No, I've got to go.' She whirled and ran for the safety of her home.

'Lunch, Lani?' Dake asked her on Thursday. 'If we're going to Washington next Wednesday on the Sorenson matter, I'd like a crash course on the whole situation.'

Lani's mind went blank. In the last few days she had barely seen Dake. Now, out of the blue, he wanted lunch. She remembered his comment on how she always refused him, but could not come up with a single reason to decline.

'Fine,' she said, finally. 'Are you ordering in?'

'Yes, deli sandwiches. Want a Coke?'

She nodded, already nervous at the idea of sharing an intimate lunch for two in his office or hers. She had tried to be busy all week to avoid him. The past weekend had shown her how dangerous it was to be with Dake Morgan.

She switched on her secretary's intercom. 'Stacey, get me the files on the Sorenson matter; Dake and I'll be reviewing them at noon. Also, that article in *Business Week* and the prospectus we found from McMasters.' She was in control, in her area of business. Why couldn't she be in control of her personal life as well?

Shortly after noon, Lani presented herself at Dake's office, the catered lunch already served. He was sitting behind his desk, talking on the phone. At his nod, she came in and moved to sit in the visitor's chair.

She glanced around the office while he finished his conversation. He had not made any changes to the way Peter had had it. The walls were the same muted grey, the carpet maroon, the big walnut desk dominated the space before the window. The pictures on the walls were different, however: the sailing boats that had been Peter's love were gone. In their places were landscape scenes, wild, stormy ocean views, high cliffs and ragged crags of soaring mountains. All first-class oils, exciting, limitless, free.

He hung up the phone, his attention all on Lani.

She smiled politely, nodding to the stack of papers in her arms. 'There's a lot to go over.'

'Let's get started.' He rose and closed the door, moving the tray of food to his desk. Taking the stack of folders from Lani, he put them on the desk and drew her up. Without a word, he leaned down and kissed her gently.

'You've been working very hard this week, mostly at avoiding me. Why?' His tone was gentle, coaxing.

She blinked, tried to look away from his penetrating gaze to gather her thoughts from this unexpected embrace, to ignore the surge of longing that coursed through her body. His hands were warm and firm on her arms, his eyes steady and dark.

'Not avoiding you, exactly,' she hedged, trying to pull back. 'Just busy.'

'Had nothing to do with our picnic or the dance or Sunday?'

She licked her lips. 'No, of course not.'

'Of course not. Lani, you've got to move on, let the past go and give the future a chance.'

She was silent a long moment, then nodded her head. 'I know. I am moving on.'

'Umm, then how about dinner tomorrow?'

Panicked, she looked up. She didn't want to see him alone. Not just yet. How to refuse?

'No refusal accepted. We'll go some place quiet. Can you get a sitter for Annalise?'

'I guess so.'

'Do you want to go dancing?'

Instantly the image of them dancing at the Sorenson ball flashed into her mind. Her body said yes, her mind shouted no! She did not need that temptation. Slowly she shook her head.

'In fact, I think you should come to dinner at my place. I'll cook. Do you like chicken *cacciatora*?' She would feel more in control if they were at her place; she would have things to do, could escape any dangerous situation.

'Yes. I'd like anything you prepared. When?'

'Sevenish?' She suddenly felt light and free. Maybe, once she was clear on the past, she could see what the future held. Would there be any future between Dake and her? Could she ever let herself trust him again?

He smiled and nodded, kissing her lightly, then turned to unpack the lunch.

As they ate, he quizzed her on the background of the Sorenson investigation, the problems they experienced, what steps Sanderson's had taken to uncover the illegal activities in the hostile take-over, the earlier Congressional committee meetings.

'It seems like an open and shut case,' he mused after two hours.

'It seemed so to me, but once at the committee the opposition was clever in twisting things, minimising wrongdoing, altering how we viewed certain aspects, until you would have thought it a minor matter. I thought we would have a resolution before now.'

'So you think we have gone as far as we can go on our end?'

'Yes, I do. Short of subpoenas or spies in their organisation, I don't think we can get any further information.'

'On the surface I tend to agree with you, but I have a couple of contacts you might not have touched, that might turn up something else. Stephanie's father, for one.'

Of course, he had contacts she'd never aspire to. It was a tight community, the high finance arena—maybe he would come up with more. Still, her team had garnered a lot of information, more than John had thought they would. Good, useful information that had helped their client at the last set of hearings. She would not be ashamed of her work; she'd done a good job.

A knock on the door interrupted. Lani looked up, surprised to see how late it was. Mark opened at Dake's command and stepped in, a sheaf of papers in his hands.

'Time for the review?' he asked.

'Yes, come on in; Lani and I were reviewing the Sorenson matter. Mark has the final project figures for Forscue. Want to stay?'

'Sure.' They were back to business.

Lani left work a little early the next day, Friday, picking up Annalise and dropping her at home before going to the market. She wanted Annalise to dust and pick up any of her things that were on the first floor before Dake arrived.

Anticipating only a few minutes at the market, she left Annalise on her own and dashed out. Lani was on her way home, when she was caught in a massive traffic jam due to a multi-car accident. As the minutes ticked by, Lani's impatience grew. She did not like to leave Annalise alone for long. Dake would be arriving soon, and she still had dinner to prepare. Traffic was at a total standstill!

Anxiously she searched for a way to turn around, to turn off the street to try another. But there was no way; she was locked in. The drivers around her seemed just as frustrated and angry, and unable to move. It was Friday night; everyone wanted to get home.

Her second-hand moved relentlessly along as the hour advanced: six-thirty, six forty-five, five past seven. Lani could have screamed with frustration; she had so much to do, was nervous, anyway, with Dake's visit, and had wanted to greet him calmly, with dinner prepared. Instead, he'd be there first, she was still in her work clothes and nothing was prepared for dinner.

Finally the cars inched ahead, slowly at first, gradually picking up speed. She could see the path the police had cleared, squeezed through the opening, and was able to drive normally at long last. She made it home in record time after that, but long after Dake was due.

Dake's beaten-up old jeep was parked in front. Naturally he would not be late.

She grabbed the bags of groceries and hurried to let herself in.

'Mommy, Mommy, it's him! It's him, the man in your secret box!'

Lani opened the door to the warmth of her apartment only to find Annalise dashing over to her, Dake seated on the sofa.

'Mommy, it's him!' Annalise was dancing before her, her eyes shining, her voice excited. She grabbed her mother's arm and pulled her towards the sofa.

Dazed, Lani let the bags of groceries sink to the carpet, while her stunned eyes looked at the scene before her.

On the coffee-table, spread before Dake Morgan, were the few pitiful mementoes she had of her marriage to him. The few pictures, the brief love notes, his class ring which she had used as a wedding-ring. All spread out before him.

CHAPTER ELEVEN

LANI raised shocked eyes and stared into Dake's angry gaze.

'It seems we knew each other before,' he said tightly.

She sank into the chair opposite, looked at Annalise.

'What is the meaning of this? Why did you go into my box?' *Why did you show the contents to Dake*? she screamed internally. She didn't know what to do. How would he react? Why had it come out, and tonight of all nights?

Annalise sensed something wrong. 'I'm sorry, Mommy. But I remembered why I thought Dake looked familiar to me. I got the box to see if I was right and I was. Then I showed him and he wanted to see what else was in the box. I told him it was your secret box.' Annalise hung her head and darted a quick glance at Dake.

His eyes bore into Lani, deep, dark, and angry. His lips were thin lines, a muscle jerked in his cheek as he clenched his jaw. Anger radiated from him in waves.

She shivered.

'So it seems we knew each other before,' he said again, his eyes never moving.

'Yes,' she whispered, her throat tight with fear, mesmerised by his stabbing stare as a rabbit before a rattler.

'Were we lovers?'

She looked at the pictures. Could you tell that from them? Or was it a lucky guess, an intuitive knowing?

His eyes swivelled to Annalise, analysing, assessing. 'And Annalise is my daughter.' He stated it, didn't ask.

'Yes.' Lani couldn't lie. It was not how she wanted the truth known, by either of them, but she couldn't lie.

'I wanted to give your daughter something of yours, since I couldn't give her a father. I remembered you were fond of your mother, so I named Annalise after her.'

Annalise's eyes grew large and she turned to look at Dake. 'You're my daddy? Why did you leave us? Why didn't you stay and help us?' she asked accusingly.

'Interesting question, isn't it?' he said, almost pleasantly. 'Maybe I wasn't given the option to stay.'

'Don't tell me that! You walked out on me! Do you know how hellish it's been? It changed my life forever.' Lani sat up, anger building within her, all the hurt and pain of the last ten years boiling over. What was he trying now? 'Without a word, not a single word. Just disappeared. I didn't know where you were, if you were even alive or dead. You just left...'

'I wouldn't have done something like that.'

'You did.'

He rubbed his forehead as if to ease the tension, and slowly his arm dropped.

'When was this?'

'April, ten years ago, as if you didn't know.'

'I don't remember,' he said.

She stared at him. How could he forget?

'You have had our daughter for ten years and I never knew. What happened ten years ago I can't speak for right now. But I've been here for weeks and you never said a word. What kind of woman are you, Lani? What kind of mother would keep a child from her father?'

She blazed into anger.

'What kind of mother am I? You have your nerve—what kind of father have you ever been? You split, without a word all these years. I tried to find you, hired detectives when I didn't have enough money for food. Ran ads when I wondered if I could keep the apartment. I tried everything I knew to find you. For months. All to no avail.'

'I don't remember.' He paused a moment, trying to drag the memory from his brain. 'You recognised me when I started at Sanderson's?'

'Yes.'

'You could have told me,' he said angrily.

'You never even acknowledged you knew me.' She should have talked to him when he first came. Found out then and there when they could have discussed things rationally. But she'd been afraid of raking things up, afraid of the emotional scene, afraid of what he would tell her.

Her stomach churned, her heart pounded and the blood roared in her ears. It couldn't have been as bad as she felt now. She should have done it when he first came.

He rubbed his forehead again. 'I thought you looked familiar; I just couldn't place you.'

She'd heard it before, but it still hurt.

He stood abruptly, towering over Lani. She shrank back in her chair, eyes fixed on Dake. With a muttered oath, he swung around and began pacing the small room. 'Ten years ago I was in a bad car crash in Chicago. I was in the hospital for weeks.' He lightly fingered the scar on his face. 'This was one memento. The other was total loss of memory. I know nothing of my life from before I awoke in that hospital. I don't remember mother, father, family, childhood. Nothing.'

Lani was appalled. How awful for him! How awful for them both. Her emotions spun; how did this change things—would it alter the past?

A thought struck. She knew little about amnesia, but she had always heard the victim was blocking unpleasant things from his or her mind. Had their marriage placed such a burden on Dake that he had had to block it out?

He swung around, anger still evident. 'Dammit, Lani, you've known me since you first saw me; why didn't you tell me? What game were you playing?'

She gave a sickly smile. 'I thought you were playing games. I had no idea you've lost your memory.'

'It's not something you tell people. It's unsettling. But I've been here for weeks; you knew who I was the moment I came into that conference-room. Why didn't you tell me? Why didn't you tell me about Annalise?'

'You have no rights to my life, to knowing anything. You have no rights to Annalise.'

'She's my daughter! My God, I've a child and you think I have no right! I want to see her, learn to know her, have her know me. I'm her father, for God's sake!'

'No,' she said quickly, too quickly. 'She's my daughter; you forfeited all rights when you walked out.'

'I forfeited nothing. You don't know a thing about what happened ten years ago.'

'I know what I went through.' Her eyes flashed and her voice was low, intense, passionate.

'You have the before to remember. I have nothing! Do you know what that means? Lani——' his voice was deadly '—I want to see her, get to know her. She's my *daughter*!'

Lani shook her head, afraid of what he might do. Afraid for herself and for her daughter.

'I want free access to her. If you fight me, I'll fight back, and for full custody.'

'No!'

'You've had her for ten years; it's my turn.'

Annalise drew near her mother. 'I don't want to go with him, Mommy, I want to stay with you.'

'Of course you will, sweetheart. He's just talking.' With a warning glance at Dake, she continued, 'People get upset with some surprises and he's just reacting right now. Of course you'll stay with me, don't you worry. Now, why don't you go into the kitchen and fix some of those cookies we made the other evening? Get some milk for all of us and we'll settle down and talk. OK?'

'OK, Mommy.' Annalise gave Lani a quick hug and ran off to the kitchen without a backward look at Dake.

'You're right, this discussion shouldn't be held before her. But, dammit, I can't believe you didn't tell me.'

'Dake, you walked out on me ten years ago. I tried to find you and never could. I knew nothing about you when you showed up at Sanderson's weeks ago. I was waiting for you to say something. You never did.'

He stooped beside her chair, his eyes on a level with hers, boring directly into hers, the anger, frustration and pain evident as he spoke clearly.

'She's my daughter, too. You must have known I would want to know her, love her.'

'No, you can't have her; you relinquished your rights years ago.' Lani's throat ached with tears. In her worst nightmares she'd never envisaged this. 'I want you to go,' she said dully. She couldn't cope any more.

He rose and looked down at her. 'Maybe you're right, for now. But I'll be back.'

She moved to the door, wanting to close it behind him, lock it, bolt it and never open it again. She almost walked into him when he suddenly stopped and turned. His hands grasped her arms, hard and angry.

'Dammit, I could slap you for not telling me weeks ago.' He looked into her eyes, now brimming with tears, and with a groan he drew her to him, punishing her with his kiss, his lips hard and hurtful, his arms drawing her against him in a tight vice. His intention was to hurt, to subjugate, to master.

Despite that, Lani felt the same attraction she'd always had for him; she wished the kiss were in love and not anger, wished they could go back ten years and start over, do whatever they had to do to make it all come right.

Her tears spilled over and ran down her cheeks. Dake felt them and drew back slowly.

His fingers traced her lips, swollen from his assault, his face contorting wryly. 'God, you're twisting me up inside!'

He flung open the door and was gone.

Lani leaned against the closed door and tried to catch her breath. She was shaking, scared and sad. What was she going to do?

Hearing Annalise coming from the kitchen, she dashed away the tears and moved towards the sofa. She sat down where Dake had been, the cushions still shaped by his body. Sadly she picked up the few pictures she had from that special time.

'I'm sorry we went into your secret box, Mommy.' Annalise put a tray of cookies and milk on the table and sat next to her mother. 'I didn't mean to make everyone angry.' Her voice was small, contrite.

'I know, sweetie, but you shouldn't go into other people's secret boxes. They're private.'

'Now I've caused a lot of trouble.'

'Yes, I think you might have. But we've faced trouble before and come through. We will this time, too. Somehow.'

'Is he really my daddy?'

'Yes, he is.'

Annalise snuggled up to her mother. 'Tell me about him,' she invited.

Lani leaned back, closed her eyes and told her daughter what she knew of Dake Morgan when she had been a young girl. Of the happy times they had had, of the things they'd done, places they had gone. She told her of his kindness, his concerns for injustice, his strong convictions to do what he thought was right.

'Even if someone does something we don't like, or has a bad trait that we wish he would change, it doesn't mean we can't love him,' Lani finished.

'And do you still love my daddy?'

Lani paused a long moment, wanting it to be different. 'Yes, I've always loved him; I probably always will. He was a very special person in my life.'

'Can't he be special again?'

'I don't know.' What had caused him to block out all memories of their time together, never remembering in ten years? She felt sick. People blocked out memories when they were too awful to deal with. Was that how he saw their mar-

riage, as so awful that he never remembered it in
ten years? Was there any feeling in him for her?
Had there ever been?

She was older now, able to stand on her own
two feet. She'd be in a better position to cope
whatever happened, yet could she stand the awful
desolation and despair she'd felt before?

She didn't think she could live through it all
again.

After Annalise was in bed, Lani sat down
before the fire to consider what she had better
do to prepare if Dake was serious in his desire to
gain custody of his daughter. He might settle for
the right to visit from time to time, but, if his
convictions were strong that he wanted her ex-
clusively for the next ten years, Lani would have
a real fight on her hands.

She knew more and more courts were allowing
children to go with their fathers, if he could
provide a good home. Which Dake could. Yet
surely the child had some say in the matter, especially when she was old enough to decide?

Even visitation rights would be hard. Lani
would see him every time he came for Annalise,
every time he dropped her off. Hear from her
daughter all they had done on their visit. Each
time the longing would be there for him to come
see her, Lani, to pick her up, spend time with
her, love her.

Lani hugged herself, the old familiar ache in
her heart threatening to overwhelm her. It was
hard, but she'd have to do what she could to
protect herself and her child. Why couldn't he

have stayed with her? Why couldn't he have loved her as she loved him?

Sunday morning the phone rang, and Lani answered.

'Lani, I want to see Annalise today.' Dake's hard voice was at the other end.

'She's not here.' Lani began to feel sick; had it begun already?

'At Judith-Ann's?' he asked.

'Yes.'

'I'll pick her up there.'

'No, you can't. She's there for the day; they're going skating and she loves that. I don't think you should try anything right away.'

'So I'll see her tonight.'

'Dake, tonight is a school night. She has to go to bed early.'

'Dammit, Lani, you're making this difficult. I want to see her.'

'Be reasonable. You don't know much about kids; she has to get a good night's sleep before school.'

'Whose fault is it that I don't know about kids?' he growled.

'Yours!' She slammed down the receiver. Taking a shaky breath, Lani gently eased the receiver up and laid it on the table. She couldn't talk with him any more.

Afraid he would come by, she quickly did the breakfast dishes and left for the mall. She'd go shopping, catch a movie, then pick up Annalise for dinner. They would not see Dake today!

CHAPTER TWELVE

LANI called in sick on Monday, not ready to face Dake, not ready to pick up the pieces of her life again, not with his awful threat hanging over her. She pretended to Annalise that she had the flu, and stayed in bed most of the day.

On Tuesday, Dake called her.

'Lani, come to work.' His voice was hard, uncompromising.

'No,' she said, about to hang up on him again.

'Wait, hear me out.' Had he known what she was planning to do? 'I want to talk to you, when we can both be rational and calm and discuss the situation. Maybe Saturday. In the meantime, we still have the trip to Washington tomorrow and you need to get back to work and get ready for that. I think I've turned up something. I need you to review it and place it in context if you can.'

He was putting their relationship back on a business level.

She sat silent, wondering if she dared trust herself to be in the same room with him. She was a professional; she had a demanding job, and was good at it. After a minute, she agreed.

'Fine, I'll expect you here after lunch.' He hung up before she could say anything. Afraid she'd raise objections?

Feeling as shaky as if she had had the flu, Lani arrived at her office shortly after eleven. At one-thirty John Harrington called her to his office.

'Dake's come up with a couple of other angles we want to review in preparation to the committee hearings tomorrow. Sorry you were ill yesterday—feeling better today?'

She nodded, feeling sick at the prospect of facing Dake Morgan again, even in John's company.

Dake was all business when he arrived, scarcely glancing her way. His facts were brief, but significant. The chief financial officer of A.I.L. International had indiscreetly written a memo about the take-over of Sorenson's and a copy had found its way into Dake's hand. He shared it with Lani and John.

'Interesting, don't you think?' he asked.

'This shows there was stock manipulation!' John exclaimed.

'That and the fact that A.I.L. signed a letter of intent with Rudolph Thompson assuring him three million dollars if he sued. The only intent being in tying up Sorenson's assets and attention while the take-over was quietly being manipulated.'

'This will make an even stronger case against them before the SEC and clear Sorenson's management entirely. No more take-over.' Lani was quick to see the ramifications.

'My thoughts exactly.' Dake was satisfied.

She refused to look at him, but she did give credit where due. 'It was good work—one of your contacts, I suppose.'

'Right. John, Lani briefed me on this situation last week. We can review it again in light of these pieces, and prove their machinations were the causes of the allegations against Sorenson's. Should be able to wrap it up in one day at the committee hearing.'

'Good. You two work on it and get the matter cleared up. I won't say anything to Sorenson's until it's closed. They will be glad when it is all over.'

'Lani, come back to my office with me and we'll go over it.'

'Couldn't it wait a while? I have things yet to do that should have been done yesterday.'

'Let's strike while the iron's hot.' Dake's voice was cool.

'All right.'

Lani walked to Dake's office like a prisoner on the way to execution. She was numb to her surroundings, numb to any feelings. She only had the nagging worry of how to keep her daughter safe from this man.

He closed the door behind her and moved to stand near his desk. She stood and watched him warily, wondering what was coming next.

'I had Stacey book our flight. We leave tomorrow morning at seven; that should get us there in plenty of time for our ten o'clock slot before the committee. We're booked on the nine p.m. flight home.'

'Why so late? The committee meeting won't last that long.'

'Thought it would give us time to have dinner, discuss the situation we find ourselves in.'

'I don't want to have dinner with you.'

'Dammit! I don't care what you want!' He took a deep breath and turned to the window. 'I swore I wouldn't get angry, I wouldn't let my temper get out of hand. But I find I couldn't get any angrier if I tried.' He rubbed his forehead, and turned back to her. 'You stand there so calm, so cool.'

'I thought we were going to talk about the Sorenson project.' She wasn't calm or cool, just numb.

'Tell me the whole story. Were you seeing other men when we were lovers? Is that the real reason your husband walked out on you, because he found out your baby wasn't his? Was your divorce because of that?'

She blinked, shocked. He still didn't know. She should tell him. She opened her mouth, then stopped. He'd been furious over Annalise, that she hadn't told him about her. How angry would he be to find out there was more she hadn't told him?

She replied only to the last. 'There was never a divorce.'

Dake looked stunned. He stared at her as if he couldn't believe his ears.

'What?' His voice was deadly quiet.

She remained still as a statue. 'There was never a divorce.' He obviously hadn't seen their marriage licence when he'd gone through the things in her box. Would that have jogged his memory?

'God,' he said, and sat in his chair as if his world had been knocked sideways.

She moved to the door.

'Lani, wait. I thought I had a solution, but this complicates things. I never suspected you hadn't got a divorce.'

She stared at the rich polished wood of the door, waiting for him to finish, wanting to leave.

'I want you to marry me.'

She turned around, her eyes wide. 'Is this a trick?'

'No, I think it's a solution. You've thrown a monkey-wrench into it, but that's just a matter of time. I want you to marry me.'

'Why, so you have rights to Annalise without having to fight for them?'

'If you like.'

'What else could there be?' She held her breath.

He hesitated a moment, then clenched his jaw.

'There is no other reason right now. I thought there might be a week ago, but I was wrong.'

'No, Dake, I won't marry you. It would be hellish!' She yanked open the door and fled down the hall. Slamming the door to her own office, she made sure it was locked before she burst into tears.

'Lani, are you all right?' Stacey was knocking on the door.

Reluctantly Lani opened it. 'No, I think I'm still suffering the after-effects of the flu. I'm going home.'

'I'll drive you; you're in no state to drive yourself.' Dake stepped into her office before she could shut the door.

'No, I'll...'

'No argument. Stacey, get her bag. Thanks. Come on, Lani.' With his hand firmly grasping her upper arm, she had no choice.

'My car...'

'Will be fine in the car park. I'll pick you up in the morning. You can get your car when we get back from Washington.'

'Just leave me alone,' she said as they made their way to his jeep.

'Not likely, sweetheart. Get in.'

The tears continued to trace their way down her face, and Dake impatiently thrust his handkerchief into her hand as he handed her into his jeep. Locking the door, he continued to the driver's side.

They drove in silence, but Lani was still crying when they reached her home.

'Please leave me alone,' she said tiredly, opening the door.

'I want Annalise,' he said flatly.

Lani didn't reply. Was it fair of her to deny her daughter the chance to know her father? Maybe she should offer a compromise, one she could be comfortable with, that wouldn't give Dake a reason to pursue it in the courts.

She took a shaky breath. 'Maybe she could visit you this weekend.'

He looked at her, coolly assessing the response. Nodding briefly, he agreed.

'It's a start. I'll pick you up at six tomorrow morning.'

She closed the door to the jeep carefully, walked on shaking legs to her home. She heard the jeep drive away as she closed her door. The tears started again. Would she lose her daughter to Dake? She loved her daughter, but wanted what was best for the child. Wouldn't it be better for her to stay with her mother?

At dinner Lani broached the subject of the visit.

'Dake would like you to visit him this weekend,' she said casually to Annalise.

'Are you coming?' Her daughter didn't look thrilled with the prospect.

'No.'

'Then me neither.' Annalise placidly resumed eating.

'He wants to get to know you better, spend some time with you.'

'I don't. If you go, I will, but otherwise I don't want to go.' Annalise was firm.

'Annalise....'

'You come, too, Mommy.' As the girl stared back at her mother defiantly, Lani could see her father's strength in her. Lani didn't think that was what Dake had in mind—she knew it wasn't. She'd try again later; she was too drained to discuss it further now.

Lani didn't sleep well, apprehension about the impending trip keeping her awake. Would she be able to sleep on the plane? She doubted it. There was to be no one else on this trip, no safety in numbers. Once before the SEC committee, Lani would be fine. She just had to get there.

She dressed in her navy suit and her crisp white blouse. Make-up was discreetly applied and her hair efficiently put in a French plait. She looked cool, collected. She felt slightly sick with nerves.

Dake was prompt. Lani had been watching for his jeep and let herself out when she spotted it.

'Annalise OK?' he asked as she climbed in.

'I sent to her Judith-Ann's until time for school. Her mother will see them both off.'

'Tonight?'

'Mrs Palmer will keep her overnight. You needn't play the concerned parent. I have been taking good care of her for all her life.'

Dake slammed the car in gear and roared off.

'I'll pick her up Saturday at ten.'

'She doesn't want to come,' Lani replied stiltedly.

'What?'

'She said no, not...'

'Not what?'

'Not without me,' she said resignedly.

Dake turned on to the approach to Callahan Tunnel, jockeying for position in the lane that led to Logan International.

'OK, you come, too,' he said.

'No.'

'Lani, I'm not playing games. I'll see Annalise one way or the other.'

Lani fell silent.

Once settled in their seats with the flight attendants serving coffee, Dake leaned back and closed his eyes. Lani started to relax; his attention was not on her. She was startled when he spoke.

'Tell me about Annalise. What she was like as a baby, when she learned to walk, her first words.'

She glanced at him. His eyes remained closed, his mouth a disciplined line. Slowly Lani began to talk, telling him about their baby, their little girl.

Dake remained with his eyes closed, listening to Lani's soft voice, interjecting a question here and there, requesting further information now and then.

'It must have been hard, raising a child as a single parent.'

'It was, sometimes.'

Lani remembered the times when she had had so little money that they had lived on cereal and fruit. Annalise was always fed; she herself had gone hungry once or twice. The constant worry that had plagued her of a major illness or losing her job, or not finding a baby-sitter. The clothes that they wore long after their time because she couldn't afford new ones. As a baby Annalise wore no shoes because Lani couldn't afford them.

It was behind her now. And she was stronger for having lived through it and survived. But it had not been easy.

They landed at Washington's National Airport and took a cab to the hearing. Arriving in good time for their turn before the committee, Lani explained how the procedure worked.

She served as spokesperson representing Sorenson's when called, and was articulate and succinct in her responses. Her adrenalin was flowing; she was sure of herself, certain the new information would make a significant difference.

The hearing lasted until after five. When it was adjourned, Lani was exhausted.

Dake unexpectedly complimented her on her handling of the situation.

'You were sure, decisive, yet always with a touch of deference for the committee members. They loved you.'

'Peter was my coach; he was good,' was all she said, but she was warmed by his praise.

'How about dinner at the Flagship Restaurant? They have good seafood.'

'Couldn't we change our tickets and just go home?' she asked, not meeting his eyes. 'It's been a long day and I didn't sleep well last night.'

'Guilty conscience?'

She threw him an angry look. 'No, keyed-up over this hearing. If you don't want to go back, say so. I'll get a cab.'

'We'll go.' The geniality was gone.

The return flight was strictly business, with an analysis of the hearing, the reaction to the new information, the way the opposing side had gone from cockiness to concern to consternation.

It was after eight when they arrived at Logan International. Hungry, Dake insisted they stop at McDonald's on the way to Lani's place. Hungry as she was, she was impatient to get home, to close her door on the world and be alone. The strain of the day was almost too much for her to stand.

When they reached her apartment, she took her briefcase in preparation for leaving.

Dake opened his door. 'I'll walk you in.'

'There's no need,' she said quickly. 'I'll be fine.'

He ignored her and opened her door, escorted her to the front door.

'Thanks for the ride.' She fumbled with the keys.

His warm fingers closed over hers, gently removing the keys and inserting them in the locks. Opening the door, he waited for her to enter, removed the keys and followed her in.

'Saturday,' he said, staring down at her, too close for comfort.

Lani swallowed hard and stepped back, suddenly aware of his height, his strength, how dark his eyes were.

'Annalise wants you to come, too; is that a strong sense of loyalty?'

She nodded. 'I think so. She probably got it from you—you always had a deep loyalty.'

He was quiet, his eyes fixed on Lani's. 'How well did we know each other? We were lovers—anything more?'

She nodded, unable to swallow now. She should tell him they were married. He would be angry that she had not told him the other night, but she should tell him. 'We knew each other well, I thought.'

He reached out to take her shoulders, drawing her close to him.

'It explains why you look familiar to me. I can't remember, but you seem familiar, as if the image of you is hovering just beyond what I can recall. Holding you seems right; your body fits into mine, your lips a perfect match, your hair familiar to my touch.'

He drew her against him and lowered his lips to hers. As the kiss deepened, Lani felt his hands undo the French plait, his fingers gently caressing, and her hair swirled free around her face. His fingers pushed through her hair, caressing her neck, her throat as his kiss went on and on.

Lani tried to resist; intellectually she didn't want this, but her traitorous body ignored her mind, delighting in his touch, revelling in his kiss.

Dake eased her suit jacket from her shoulders, dropping it on the floor, his followed.

'Mmm, no, Dake. Stop,' she murmured when his lips left hers to travel down her neck, to the hollow of her throat. He kissed the pulse at the base, his lips warm and caressing.

His fingers threaded in the silky strands of her hair, his hands holding her face to receive his kisses.

Lani felt the old magic she had always experienced with Dake; she was lost to time and place, floating softly on a sensuous sea of pleasure.

Her hands drew through his thick hair, moving to grasp the strong muscles of his shoulders. It felt so right, so perfect.

'Where's your room?' he asked, his voice soft.

Shocked, she tried to draw back. She didn't want this to go on. Her body was weak with longing and desire, so that, had he not been holding her, she would have fallen. But they must stop.

'No,' she whispered. 'Annalise...'

'Isn't here tonight.' He released her and took her hand, threading his fingers through hers, starting for the stairs.

'Stephanie...'

'Stop throwing her in my face all the time. Stephanie has gone back to New York and I don't expect to see her again.'

Pulling her up the stairs, he paused at the top. A brief gesture by Lani indicated her room. When he entered, he paused a moment to survey the neat room, eyeing the double bed. Smaller than he was used to, but it would suffice.

'Dake, don't do this to me,' she objected, trembling with emotions. One part yearned unbearably to recapture the love they had shared, another part argued this was a big mistake.

'I'm not doing anything to you; we're doing it together.'

His mouth descended on hers, driving out all thought, all awareness. There were only feelings left, wondrous, glorious, mindless feelings.

His hand roamed over her body, moulding hers to his, setting her nerve-endings tingling as he made her his.

Lani gasped in surprise when he released the fastener of her bra. She had not been aware that he had unbuttoned her blouse. His hands moved slowly, agonisingly slowly from caressing her back, to her side to caress the soft swell of her breasts. Aching for him to complete the journey, she shifted positions to grant him greater access.

'Slowly, sweetheart—are we in a hurry?' Dake spoke softly, gazing down into her silvery eyes with warm brown ones, his gaze dropped to feast on her beauty.

Trembling with desire, passion and impatience, Lani moved closer, moved against him, wanting more.

Yes, she was in a hurry; she wanted it all, now.

His hands continued their long journey, finally cupping her breasts, his thumbs gently fondling the taut, thrusting nipples.

Lani moaned involuntarily as the delight pervaded her body, anticipation built, passion flared. She caught her breath at the exquisite pleasure his touch brought.

Unbuttoning his shirt with numb fingers, she tugged it off, trying to ignore the sensations his mouth caused. She ran her hands across his chest, tracing the warm skin, the solid wall she remembered. Moving slowly down, she slipped her fingers behind the belt, then tugged at the belt buckle.

'You are impatient,' Dake murmured, straightening and assisting her.

In only a moment they were disrobed and he swept her up in his arms, laying her on the bed. Immediately he followed her down, his mouth capturing her, his hands learning the secret places of her body, trailing fire in their wake.

Lani sank against the mattress, revelling in his touch, long-forgotten pleasures crowding her senses as his hands moved to find, to entice, to tantalise, to satisfy. His lips captivated her, his tongue tasting the sweetness of her mouth, the satiny skin of her throat, her breasts. The hot moistness enchanted Lani as she focused on each exquisite touch, her body quivering in response.

She grew more feverish with each passing moment, her hands holding Dake, his skin warm beneath her fingers, the texture of his body quickly relearned. She relished the strength of his back, the breadth of his shoulders, the narrow waist, savoured the sensation she experienced when moving her hands over him, touching where she wanted, free to satisfy her yearnings.

The enchanting budding within her grew and expanded, threatening to take over her life. She drew his head up, seeking his mouth with her lips, wanting to give herself to this man, to find the paradise only he could provide her.

Dake moved to trail fiery kisses down her throat, down across her shoulders, to the soft swell of her breasts.

Lani ached with tormenting pleasure, her whole being flooded with love for this man, love for his touch, the enchantment he brought.

His mouth moved lower, trailing fire and heat in its wake. His tongue encircled her navel, plunged into its recess.

Lani arched to meet him, moving to find him.

'Easy, baby, there's time,' he murmured, continuing his ministrations.

'Oh, God! Please, Dake, I want you so much,' she panted, gasping for breath, her body on fire for him.

One hand fondled her breast while the other continued its wanderings; his mouth wreaked sweet havoc between as he tasted her, caressed her, his lips touching every inch of skin.

Lani thought she would explode.

Endless hours of delight, of delicious enjoyment, of exploding passion passed. Lani was mindless with yearning, the bloom of desire engulfing her, maddening her so that her only thought was for Dake. She wanted him so damn much!

When he moved, Lani became still, in awe at the churning feelings which threatened to rip her asunder. She could feel him move, feel his lips on hers, then she lost track of individual sensations as her body became a mass of pulsating ecstasy.

The pleasure was intense; it rolled through her body in waves, each one overwhelming, building, building. When it ebbed, she rested only a moment before it began again, stronger than before.

Panting with happiness, tired beyond all memory, she at long last lay quiet. It had been glorious.

Dake rained soft kisses on her face, her lips, her eyelids, cheeks, back to her warm lips.

Struggling to keep awake, she smiled sleepily up at him, her hands still on his back, the strong muscles playing beneath her fingers.

'How could I ever forget something like that?' he asked softly in her ear, kissing the lobe, the soft skin of her neck.

Instantly all happiness fled as she was recalled to the dilemma that faced them. How could she have permitted herself to be caught up in this? She turned her head, tears threatening.

Dake forced her head around to meet his eyes.

'Marriage to me wouldn't be all bad,' he said.

'You only want me because of Annalise,' she said dully, hoping he would deny it, longing for him to deny it, hoping he would say he loved her.

'I'm furious at the circumstances that prevented my knowing my daughter. And that you didn't tell me as soon as I arrived. But that anger will pass. When it does, we have a chance for marriage. Tonight shows us we could have something.'

'I don't know, Dake. Why don't you just leave me alone?' she said, jerking her head from his grasp.

'Think on it, Lani.' His voice was hard again, cold.

He moved off her, got up. She could hear him don his clothes, but she kept her face turned from him, willing him to leave. She didn't want a marriage just so that he had access to Annalise. But would it be better than never seeing him again? Better than letting him marry someone like Stephanie?

His hands came down on her shoulders, raised her to a sitting position, her hair soft against his fingers, her skin warm and silky.

'Think on it, Lani. I want Annalise, and I want you.' He leaned over and kissed her gently, drawing the covers to her. 'Go to sleep now; I'll let myself out.'

She lay back down, listening to his tread as he left. Tears started again when she heard the door close.

CHAPTER THIRTEEN

ON SATURDAY Lani awoke to the sound of rain. She rolled over to peer out of her window. It was a steady, drizzling rain, with no wind. Sighing, she rolled back. Today she and Annalise were going out with Dake. Not because he wanted her along, but because that was the only way he could get Annalise.

The dreary day reflected the dreary mood within. She pondered the situation from various angles. There didn't seem to be an easy way out of the problem.

Dake was still mad at her. He saw only that Lani knew him where he knew her not, and had not told him about their child. She wondered what his reaction would be if he found out they had been married. Were still married, for all that.

She didn't know Dake now. The years had changed him; they had gone their separate ways and she had changed as well. Did they have anything in common that would bind them together? He had mentioned marriage, though only for expediency's sake. She didn't know him enough to be married to him. They were strangers, with only a shared few months a long time ago.

Annalise was eating cereal when Lani went down to the kitchen. She was dressed and her hair brushed. Lani had dressed in jeans and a silvery grey pullover that matched her eyes. She had on more make-up than usual in an attempt to erase the signs of strain she had detected when looking in the mirror.

'Hi, honey. Already eating breakfast?'

'Hi, Mommy. I just wanted cereal and I didn't know when you would get done in the shower. Do we have to go today?'

Lani paused, continued her preparations for coffee.

'Yes. I'm sure Dake has already planned something.' She wished they could miss it. She worried about the consequences from him if she tried to duck out, though. This way, she had some control over the outing, over his time with Annalise. To fight him could be disastrous. She would try this way, while at the same time trying to calculate a way to make sure Annalise would be safe.

'I don't want to go,' Annalise said in a small voice.

'We'll have a good day.' Lani tried to sound cheerful despite her own disquiet. 'He would never do anything to hurt you, honey. He's your father.'

'I don't want to go with him. I want to stay with you.'

'But I'll be there, too. We'll be like a family, for today.' Even as Lani said the words, the falseness of it struck her. They would be a family bound in blood ties only; none of the love and joy of a family would travel with them today.

Gazing at her daughter, she could feel her fear. Her safe, sheltered world had been shattered. Annalise did not know what to expect and clung to her mother for the safety she sought.

Damn Dake for bringing this to their child. She would speak to him alone some time today and let him know what harm he was already causing. Would he care? Or was he so caught up in wanting what he considered his to care how the object of his quest felt?

They were ready when he knocked. Lani opened the door, the cold, damp air poured in around him. Dake stepped inside and looked at Lani, his eyes hard and cold. No sign of Wednesday's gentle lover. Glancing around, he spotted Annalise.

'Hi, Annalise,' he said, his face softening.

She muttered a hi and fled to her mother's side, reaching for Lani's hand. Standing partly behind Lani, she solemnly stared back at Dake.

He clenched his jaw, a muscle twitching in his cheek. His smouldering glance speared Lani.

'Are you ready?' he asked.

'As we'll ever be,' she replied coolly. 'Where are we going?'

'I thought we could take a drive. I wasn't expecting the rain. It's late for the leaves, but there may be some colour left. There's a museum at Concord. Thought we could stop there and go to Lexington. Return to my place later.'

'We'll carry raincoats, then.' She went to the closet to collect the rain gear, Annalise tagging along only a foot behind her mother. Dake stood by the door.

As Annalise scrambled into his jeep, his hand was hard on Lani's arm.

'What have you been telling her, to have her so stand-offish?' he murmured for her ears alone.

She looked at him in surprise. 'I had to tell her nothing. You caused that reaction.'

'Me?'

She glanced quickly at Annalise; she was not paying any attention. Lani looked back at Dake.

'You're threatening all she has ever known. You have taken from her the security in her life that she took for granted. She doesn't know you and you come in and threaten to take her away from all she's ever known. How would you feel? You must be very like your father!'

She jerked her arm free and climbed into the jeep, tugging the door shut.

Dake stood staring at her for a long moment, the rain falling on his head, running in rivulets down his cheeks.

He moved to climb into the jeep, silent, angry.

The wipers cleared the windscreen as they drove along the wet streets. The river Charles was grey and rain-spattered as they drove beside it, crossing the old bridge to Cambridge, turning towards Concord.

Lani looked out of her window at the old houses, the manicured yards, and the grey day. How many hours would they have to be with Dake? Would the day get any better? She compared it to the day they had gone on the picnic—

was it only a couple of weeks ago? How excited they had been, looking forward to a fun time. The contrast was dramatic. No one was happy on this ride; no one looked forward to the outing.

Why was he forcing the issue? Would this outing show him that he could not demand that Annalise love him, could not demand she want to be with him? Or would he keep pressing the issue?

What alternatives did she have? Maybe on Monday she could consult a lawyer and find out.

As they took the curve around Walden's Pond, Lani was again surprised at how large it was. Where she was from, a pond was a small body of water; this was more like a lake to her.

'Have you been here before?' Dake asked, his eyes seeking Annalise in the mirror.

'Once or twice. Do you remember, Annalise?' Lani answered.

'No.' She scooted over in the seat, to avoid Dake's eyes.

Lani turned to look back out the window, a smile tugging at her mouth. Maybe she didn't need to worry about her daughter, after all. Maybe Annalise could take care of herself.

'I don't know if I've been here, but I sure don't remember,' he said.

'You don't remember anything?' It was still hard to believe.

'Nothing of a personal nature. Not family, nor friends, nor places where I might have lived. I remember how to read, calculate, dates in history. Things you learn in school.'

Lani suddenly felt sad for him. It must be awful to wake up and not know who you were. How frightening. A person would be so helpless, dependent solely on those around him for information. He would depend on the people he trusted to tell him who he was, what had happened, everything.

'And you remember nothing of Boston?'

'Now that I'm here, sometimes I see something and know I've seen it before. But I don't know when, or if anyone was with me.'

'Why can't you remember?' Annalise asked, leaning forward in her seat to hear better.

'I don't know, sweetheart. I wish I could remember. I just can't.' His voice with Annalise was gentle, none of the harshness he used with Lani.

'Is that why you never came back to Mommy and me, because you didn't remember we were there?'

'I can think of no other reason, Annalise.'

Lani's eyes filled with tears, and her heart ached for them. They had been so in love, had thought the world stretched out ahead of them. She had never thought of Dake's point of view in all this. How awful to have that blank space there forever, never remembering.

She looked out of the window. She had to tell him. And he would be angry again that she hadn't told him long before. Or even the other evening. She didn't want to ruin the day; they had a truce of sorts. Would telling him end that? She

wouldn't risk another scene before Annalise.
She'd wait, and tell him another time.

Dake turned into the gravelled car park across
from the path to the famous Concord Bridge and
cut the engine. The rain continued steadily, but
there was no wind.

'Are we game?' he asked, staring out of the
window at the wet day.

'The raincoats will keep us dry. Put yours on,
Annalise.'

In only a moment, they were walking up the
wide pathway to the wooden bridge immor-
talised by Emerson's poem. The granite
monument to the Minutemen stood sentinel
before it. Lani stopped to read the bronze plaque,
then moved across the wooden bridge, her im-
agination spinning with remembered stories of
the war, imagining how the farmers felt as the
British soldiers approached, threatening their way
of life. It must have felt much as she felt with
Dake.

They toured the small museum, Annalise enchanted with the miniature diorama of the
battleground and towns from 1775. Dake treated
Lani courteously, watching Annalise as she went
from exhibit to exhibit.

They drove to Lexington and ate lunch in a
small coffee-shop. Dake tried to draw Annalise
out, but she responded as briefly as possible to
his questions. She stayed near Lani and would
not offer the friendliness Dake was so obviously
trying to attain. Lani tried to encourage her to
be more friendly, but to no avail.

When they had seen their fill, Dake headed back to Boston.

'I rented a couple of movies. Thought we could order something in and watch them,' he said as he drove competently through the busy streets.

'Then can we go home?' Lani asked. The day was a strain. She was already exhausted and it was only late afternoon.

'Yes, then you can go home.' Dake's voice was heavy, sad.

Lani looked at him, but his face was impassive as he negotiated the traffic.

When they reached Dake's apartment, Lani studied the living-room as if searching for clues to what made the man tick. It was tastefully decorated but no signs of knick-knacks or pictures. A pleasant room but without any personality. Did Dake keep his personal things in his bedroom? She had not seen anything in his study when they'd worked here.

Dake settled Annalise before the TV with a tape of *Cinderella*. Motioning to Lani, he went into the kitchen. She followed.

'What would Annalise like for dinner?'

'She's not a picky eater—anything would be fine.'

'Chinese?'

'Yes.' Lani moved to return to the living-room but Dake reached out and grasped her hand, threading his fingers through hers, his touch warm, exciting. Lani felt a stir in her heart. She turned back, a question in her look.

'Lani, what was my father like? Did you know him?'

'Both our parents were dead when we met. You were a big, brash graduate student on some grant; I was on a work study programme. I had a little money from my aunt and had to work to make up the rest. But you told me about your father. He was ruthless, manipulative, power-hungry. You didn't like what he had been; you were going to be different.'

'And you don't think I am?'

Dark shadows circled his eyes. For a moment Lani thought she saw pain in their depths.

She looked away, around the spotless, sterile kitchen. No, she didn't think he was, normally, but he acted that way about Annalise.

'What about my mother?' He changed the subject.

'You were fond of her. Annalise is named after her.'

His thumb rubbed the back of her hand, gently, sensuously, his eyes locked on their linked fingers.

Lani didn't move, held her breath. His touch sent sparks up her arm, down her spine. She didn't trust him, didn't know if she ever would again. But her body clamoured for his. If she could forget her past, forget everything but the exquisite delight only his touch brought, she would never leave his side.

He looked up, his eyes catching hers, holding hers, searing her. The heat rose in her until she was hot and breathless. Her eyes widened. Did she see what Dake felt, or only what she so desperately wanted to see?

He ran his free hand through his hair. 'All I want is a chance to get to know my daughter. I didn't even know I had one, and now that I do, I want to know her, have her know me.'

'I wouldn't keep you from visiting her, but you can't storm in and demand she go with you. First of all, you've frightened her, secondly, you can't demand love. Finally, I wouldn't let you.'

A glimmer of a smile touched his mouth as he gazed down at her. 'You're all fight, that's for sure. Could I take you on?'

'Don't try.' Fear beat in her heart. Could she prevail if he took her on? There was more to Dake Morgan than she could handle.

'I want my daughter, any way I can get her.'

'Including marriage to me?'

'Yes.'

'It wouldn't work.' She wanted him to deny it, convince her it would.

'Why not?'

Lani closed her eyes; they had thought it would work at one time. She had been deliriously happy for four wonderful months. But things were different now. She opened her eyes and shook her head.

'I want Annalise, and I want you.' Dake's voice was low.

'For Annalise.'

'Maybe.'

He tugged her hand and drew her closer, his lips closing on hers. Lani clung to him as his embrace went on and on, passion flaring, desires rampant. Would he love her again?

'Mommy! Come and see the show.'

The spell was broken; the threat remained. Lani drew back, searched Dake's eyes for a clue to his thoughts, but they were hard, giving nothing away.

Slowly Lani moved back and turned to the living-room.

Dake took them home after dinner. Lani was relieved. The day had been full of tension, full of strain. She wanted to find some peace.

Annalise hunched in the corner of the back seat. She'd been polite to Dake, but not forth-coming. She made it clear she would not easily be won over.

When he dropped them off, he did not get out of the car, but bade them a quiet goodnight. His face stark, remote, defeated.

Lani felt a pang. He looked so lonely, so alone. What did he have? No family, no memories, nothing but work. It was not enough.

She could change that. She could risk herself in love and offer to include him in her life, in her family. They could become the family they had planned so long ago. She could offer him com-panionship, a daughter and love.

She bade him goodnight, her thoughts spinning, her heart thumping with confusion. She loved him, but she was afraid.

CHAPTER FOURTEEN

WHEN Lani awoke the next morning, she still felt exhausted. She had spent a sleepless night, tossing and turning, worrying over what she should do. Dake's face as she had last seen it haunted her. Could she erase that look? Replace it with the happiness she'd seen at the beach, the passion at the Sorenson ball?

She was at a crossroads and it was up to her. She could take the solution Dake offered and make the best of it, or fight him every step of the way.

She sighed. The simplest solution would be his. She loved Dake, ached with wanting him to love her. To find herself in his arms each night would be heaven. Would he ever love her? Would he ever want anything more from her than to have Annalise's mother so he could have Annalise?

There was no denying she loved him. She had always loved him. There was a risk. He could leave again.

But he could stay. What if this time he stayed? All of life was a risk. Could she gamble all for the chance of happiness again?

Lani dressed slowly in grey wool trousers and a warm blue sweater. A firm, cool resolve settled over her. She would go to Dake's, talk to him. Risk everything. Her heart began pounding. She would not be deterred. Determined in what she was going to do, Lani ate a good breakfast, dropped Annalise off at Judith-Ann's and called a cab to take her to Dake's. She was too nervous to drive herself.

She had made up her mind. For good or ill, she would take marriage. She loved him. It would be better to be with him than apart. It might be awful at first, until he got over his anger, but she already knew it was hellish without him. Given time, maybe things would come right. Wasn't it worth a chance, worth the risk? She had never loved another man the way she loved Dake, and never would. Sometimes they got on well, or had in the early weeks. Eventually they could work things out. They had to.

Lani was nervous when she arrived, but she took a deep breath and rang the bell, a tentative smile on her face as Dake opened the door. Could he hear the pounding of her heart? What if he had changed his mind?

'Hello, Dake.' God, she was scared, her voice shaky, her knees weak as jelly.

'Lani, what are you doing here?'

'I came to talk to you. And to accept your offer, if it's still open,' she said in a rush, afraid to delay.

He didn't respond right away and her heart sank. Had he changed his mind?

'Come on in.' Dake watched her through narrowed eyes. She ducked her head and entered, following him into the living-room.

Where to begin? He stood watching her with an expressionless mask, giving her no support, no help, no encouragement. Lani took a deep breath.

'I know now about your amnesia. I always wondered why you left one day and never returned. If you don't remember, then we will probably never know. I'm so sorry, Dake, it must be awful!'

'You didn't come here just to tell me that.'

'No, to explain something else to you. To try to make you see why I didn't tell you earlier. Do you know I was disowned by my aunt? When my husband left, she thought I'd made up the story about being married. She thought that I was an unwed mother. To her that was as bad as you could get. From that day on she had nothing to do with me. She died about a year later. She was all the family I had.'

Dake's face softened slightly, and he took a step closer, but Lani held up her hand, shaking her head. If he was at all nice to her now she might not be able to go on.

'Do you know I almost lost the baby from poor nutrition, because I was so broke I could only eat once a day? She was born in the charity ward of Boston Hospital. I was on welfare for six months. There were times when I had to leave her alone and unattended while I worked at a job paying minimum wage, because I couldn't afford a sitter.'

'God, Lani.' Dake's eyes were filled with agony as he listened to her soft voice list the hard times

she'd gone through. 'Oh, honey.' He reached out
to draw her into his arms, but she stepped back.

'Do you know how much I loved you?' she
cried out to him. 'How many long, lonely nights
I cried myself to sleep because you'd left me, left
me and not even had the courtesy to say
goodbye.'

'But I didn't——'

'I know that now; you've explained it with the
amnesia. But for ten years that was what I
thought. I thought that and still loved you. I
thought I was over you, finally, years ago. But
the minute you walked through the door into that
meeting, I knew I'd been lying to myself. I still
loved you.'

'Thank God for that.' Dake drew her slowly
into his arms, holding her tightly, afraid to let
her go, resting his cheek against her hair as Lani
savoured the feel of his strong body against hers.
She closed her eyes. She was where she wanted
to be. Back with Dake, safe, loved. Was it a
dream?

'But I'm afraid, so afraid. You left me once—
what would stop you again? I just couldn't live
through it again,' she murmured against his chest.

'My poor Lani. Love, what a hellish time you
had. I had no idea. I don't know how I got to
Chicago, why I was going there. Only circumstances brought me back to Boston.' His arms
tightened. 'What if I had never come back? Oh,
my dearest love, how can I make it up to you?'

'I don't think it can be made up. I couldn't
understand what kind of game you were playing.

You always seemed so sincere about meeting me somewhere, always looked puzzled. But I didn't see how you could have forgotten me. I thought you were playing some dark game. I never thought of amnesia. I was shocked when you told me.'

'And I guess I've grown used to it. The doctors told me I might never remember. Major head trauma, they called it, but I'd be fine. Only I'm not and it drives me crazy sometimes. I'll have flashes of things that seem familiar, as if I've seen it before, but I can't remember when or where.'

'Yet you remembered your name,' she said, still snuggled as close to him as she could get.

'I hitched a ride with someone. He told the cops my name. It was his car that crashed. He was pretty badly hurt, too.'

'Why were you in Chicago?'

'I don't know. I hitched a ride in Massachusetts, fell asleep and woke up in the hospital in Chicago.'

She hugged him tighter, unable to say anything to make the past different. She could only hold on to him now, knowing the future would be different.

He pushed her back a little, to look down into her silvery eyes.

'And just where does your husband fit into all this?'

'I was never, ever unfaithful to my husband,' she said in a low voice.

He stared at her as realisation dawned. Closing his eyes in pain, he said softly, 'Oh, hell! My poor Lani.'

Tears welled and spilled over. 'I missed you so.'

'God, for ten years I've tried to remember who I was, what I was, anything. Do you know how awful it is not knowing anything? I have no memories of childhood, none of my family, none of you!'

His thumbs wiped the tears from her cheeks. 'Shall we try again?' he asked softly, his eyes a warm velvety brown.

She nodded. 'That's why I came today. I figured being married to you would be better than not being with you. Even if you didn't want to marry me except to get Annalise.'

He looked uncomfortable.

'Actually, that was only part of the reason. If you will think back to Sorenson's ball, you might have a clue that I was interested in you. In fact, I have wanted you ever since we met in that conference-room weeks ago. But first you were elusive, then threw Stephanie at me, then I found out about Annalise and that you had known all along and hadn't told me. I was angry.'

'Even then,' she smiled through her tears, 'I loved you.'

'And even when I was angry with you, I could only think of ways to get you to come to me. I thought marriage would be the perfect solution. I'd get my daughter, and the woman I desired.

The anger would fade, I knew. And I wanted you with me through the years. All these past years I never wanted to marry anyone, though not for want of trying by some enticing women.'

She wrinkled her nose at him. 'But you fought them off.'

'It never felt right until you.' He kissed her softly.

'When you came to Sanderson's, I was so shocked, then confused. When I found out about the amnesia, I wanted to tell you but I was afraid. Especially after some of the things you said when you found out about Annalise.'

Dake shook his head. 'I didn't know what I was thinking. I would never hurt you. Annalise is adorable and I already love her. Almost as much as I love her mother.'

Lani's heart threatened to explode with happiness.

'I was devastated when you told me there had been no divorce. Now, I thank God.' He eased her jacket off her shoulders. 'So if we were to find ourselves in a warm embrace, it would probably be all right.' His lips trailed fire as he moved across her cheeks, to her forehead, dropping to her waiting lips.

As she started on the buttons of his shirt, slanting a sultry, sexy smile up at her husband, Lani answered, 'It probably would be wonderful!'

'I love you, Lani Morgan. I will never forget that, as long as we live!'

He leaned over to kiss her again before scooping her up in his arms to carry her to heaven.

Next Month's Romances

Each month you can choose from a world of variety in romance with Mills & Boon. Below are the new titles to look out for next month, why not ask either Mills & Boon Reader Service or your Newsagent to reserve you a copy of the titles you want to buy – just tick the titles you would like to order and either post to Reader Service or take it to any Newsagent and ask them to order your books.

Please save me the following titles:		Please tick	√
PAST LOVING	Penny Jordan		
WINTER OF DREAMS	Susan Napier		
KNIGHT TO THE RESCUE	Miranda Lee		
OUT OF NOWHERE	Patricia Wilson		
SECOND CHANCE FOR LOVE	Susanne McCarthy		
MORE THAN A DREAM	Emma Richmond		
REVENGE	Natalie Fox		
YESTERDAY AND FOREVER	Sandra Marton		
NO GENTLEMAN	Kate Walker		
CATALINA'S LOVER	Vanessa Grant		
OLD LOVE, NEW LOVE	Jennifer Taylor		
A FRENCH ENCOUNTER	Cathy Williams		
THE TRESPASSER	Jane Donnelly		
A TEMPTING SHORE	Dana James		
A LOVE TO LAST	Samantha Day		
A PLACE OF WILD HONEY	Ann Charlton		

If you would like to order these books from Mills & Boon Reader Service please send £1.70 per title to: Mills & Boon Reader Service, P.O. Box 236, Croydon, Surrey, CR9 3RU and quote your Subscriber No:..(If applicable) and complete the name and address details below. Alternatively, these books are available from many local Newsagents including W.H.Smith, J.Menzies, Martins and other paperback stockists from 14th August 1992.

Name:...

Address:...

....Post Code:.......................

To Retailer: If you would like to stock M&B books please contact your regular book/magazine wholesaler for details.

You may be mailed with offers from other reputable companies as a result of this application. If you would rather not take advantage of these opportunities please tick box ☐

4 FREE

Romances
and 2 FREE gifts
just for you!

You can enjoy all the
heartwarming emotion of true love for FREE!
Discover the heartbreak and the happiness, the emotion and
the tenderness of the modern relationships in
Mills & Boon Romances.

We'll send you 4 captivating Romances as a special offer from
Mills & Boon Reader Service, along with the chance to have
6 Romances delivered to your door each month.

Claim your FREE books and gifts overleaf...

An irresistible offer from Mills & Boon

Here's a personal invitation from Mills & Boon Reader Service, to become a regular reader of Romances. To welcome you, we'd like you to have 4 books, a CUDDLY TEDDY and a special MYSTERY GIFT absolutely FREE.

Then you could look forward each month to receiving 6 brand new Romances, delivered to your door, postage and packing free! Plus our free Newsletter featuring author news, competitions, special offers and much more.

This invitation comes with no strings attached. You may cancel or suspend your subscription at any time, and still keep your free books and gifts.

It's so easy. Send no money now. Simply fill in the coupon below and post it to - **Reader Service, FREEPOST, PO Box 236, Croydon, Surrey CR9 9EL.**

--- NO STAMP REQUIRED ---

Free Books Coupon

Yes! Please rush me 4 free Romances and 2 free gifts! Please also reserve me a Reader Service subscription. If I decide to subscribe I can look forward to receiving 6 brand new Romances each month for just £10.20, postage and packing free. If I choose not to subscribe I shall write to you within 10 days - I can keep the books and gifts whatever I decide. I may cancel or suspend my subscription at any time. I am over 18 years of age.

Ms/Mrs/Miss/Mr_____   EP31R

Address _____

_____

Postcode_____Signature _____